J Miller
Miller, Jeff
20,000 nerds under the sea

$16.99
ocn904081654
First edition.

THE NERDY DOZEN

20,000 NERDS UNDER THE SEA

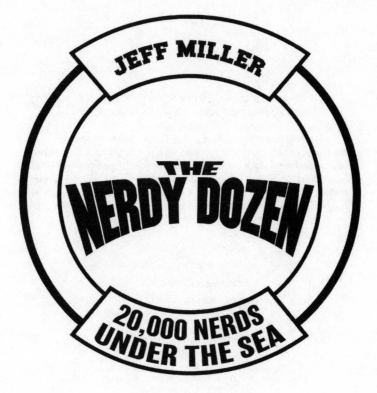

JEFF MILLER

THE NERDY DOZEN

20,000 NERDS UNDER THE SEA

HARPER
An Imprint of HarperCollinsPublishers

alloyentertainment
Produced by Alloy Entertainment
1700 Broadway, New York NY 10019

Designed by Liz Dresner
Typesetting by Elaine Damasco

Library of Congress Control Number: 2015938990
ISBN 978-0-06-227268-3

15 16 17 18 19 CG/RRDH 10 9 8 7 6 5 4 3 2 1
❖
First Edition

For "Aunt" Linda Hall—my second mom

THE NERDY DOZEN

20,000 NERDS UNDER THE SEA

"NOW, REPRESENTING COLORADO'S ROMARE SMYTHE Junior High School: Neil Andertol!" the announcer boomed to the crowded auditorium. Neil Andertol nervously stepped out from behind a heavy curtain, careful not to get tangled in the banner that read SOUTHWESTERN ROBOTICS INVITATIONAL.

He slowly walked toward the center of the stage, making sure not to break the robot he cradled in his hands.

"Good luck!" whispered a girl, Marla, who had just finished her presentation. She lugged her small, malfunctioning robotic poodle backstage. Its bark was supposed to scramble any piece of technology, but its mechanics had gone haywire halfway through.

"Thanks," mouthed Neil, his palms clammy.

He wore a blue polo shirt tucked into khaki pants. He hated tucking in his shirt—almost as much as public speaking—but somehow his family and friends had talked him into doing both.

With a thud, Neil placed his square hunk of metal on the ground. It was a flying drone, with a rotor at each of the four corners like tiny helicopter blades. Its center was a black metal hub that contained a jungle of wires, batteries, and moving parts.

The tournament host was dressed in a faded shirt and thin black necktie. His hair was shiny with hair gel, and he wore a white-and-green name tag that read AMEER.

"Who's ready for more robo fun?" Ameer asked the crowd.

The audience clapped as Neil stepped forward. He raised a hand to shield his eyes from the bright lights. Through the glare Neil looked for his family—and his friend Tyler—in the audience.

Tyler had originally meant to compete in the

tournament, but his robot had caught on fire days before. With only a pile of melted metal and ash to display, he'd convinced Neil to take his place.

Neil and his friend had created their robots as a project for their after-school robotics club, but there was one problem: each school was only allowed *one* slot in the tournament. Neil had insisted that Tyler enter, claiming that his sister had a karate tournament the same day. But really, he just wanted to see his friend succeed; and to be honest, Neil was a master video gamer, but a master with robotics? He wasn't so sure about that.

But once Tyler's robot was out of operation, there was no one to take his place but Neil.

Now, standing in front of a full auditorium, Neil ran a sweaty palm through his messy black hair. He pushed up his glasses. The lights overhead felt hotter than re-entering Earth's atmosphere.

"Neil! Over here!" shouted a voice from the crowd. It was his karate-loving younger sister, Janey. "Everyone is watching! Don't mess this up!"

"Oh, quiet, Jane. Neil, you're doing great, honey! And if it helps, I don't think everyone is watching!" shouted his mother's voice.

Oh, great.

"That's quite some cheering section you have, Neil," said the announcer, glancing at a clipboard with Neil's official entry form. "I see here you're a pretty good pilot?"

Pretty good?

"I, uh, enjoy flying things, yes," Neil said.

"Ooh, things!" said Ameer. "Any 'things' in particular?"

Neil thought about telling the truth. How past "things" he enjoyed flying included the Air Force's undercover jet fighters and NASA's experimental spacecraft—but he was sworn to secrecy.

"Just this," Neil answered, nodding to his creation lying on the stage. He'd built it using an old fan and a broken lawn mower that he'd found in his parents' garage. Several hours of online DIY-droning video demonstrations had helped with the final touches.

"Does your machine have a name?"

"Lieutenant Drones."

"I like it, very official," replied Ameer. "And this is your first time in our tournament, I see. So you *are* aware of our grand prize, yes?"

"VIP passes to attend RebootCon, and the chance to

meet Reboot Robiskie himself," Neil answered quickly.

"And there's more, folks!" said Ameer. "Don't forget about the signed photo of your meet and greet."

If there was anything that could make Neil speak in public or tuck in his shirt, it was the idea of meeting Reboot Robiskie. He was Neil's internet hero, a loner who lived on a private yacht and ran his own underground gaming site. Neil would often upload videos of his gaming to the server.

"I also see here that you are part of a club?"

"Yeah," Neil replied, leaning into the microphone. "My friend Tyler started it."

"Does it have a name?"

"Drones 'n' Scones. For people who like robots. Or baking."

"Or both!" yelled Tyler from the audience.

"Or both," Neil added. A slow laugh crept through the audience, and Neil felt his shoulders relax.

"That sounds like my kind of club," said Ameer with a phony smile. "And speaking of food, I don't want to forget to thank this year's tournament sponsor, the good people at Rogers Ketchup."

The audience gave a round of halfhearted applause.

"So without further ado, let's see what you've got, Neil," said Ameer. "Judges, are you ready? Neil, all set?"

Neil nodded.

"Neil Andertol, from Drones 'n' Scones in Colorado, you have five minutes . . . starting now!"

Neil cleared his throat and flipped a small switch on the back of his remote control. His robot came to life, loudly whirring like a facedown box fan. It slowly lifted off the ground.

"Hello, everyone," said Neil. "I'd, um, like to introduce you all to a thing I made."

Neil pushed a small remote joystick, and the drone slowly lifted higher, floating with ease. It shot across the stage, then stopped in midair, waiting for Neil's next command.

"This machine operates like most hobby drones," he continued. "While it's illegal to fly these commercially without a license, mine has a cruising altitude of a few hundred feet. Plus the controls are very responsive."

Neil pushed the joystick, and the drone dipped down. It stopped inches above the floor, pausing before it rose out toward the audience. A spotlight followed it over the crowd.

"While this drone looks simple, it does have a secret.

Who here would like a treat?" Neil asked the audience.

A young girl waved her arms from a few rows back, and Lieutenant Drones soared toward her.

"A gift from Drones 'n' Scones. Heads up!" Neil said. He pressed a button on his remote control, and a blueberry scone dropped from the center of the robot. It landed a few seats over from the intended target, but people eagerly passed the pastry to her.

"Anyone else?"

More hands were raised throughout the audience, and Neil steered his drone toward the back rows. He guided it smoothly, his tongue darting out of the corner of his mouth in concentration. Neil looked at his parents and realized it was their first glimpse at his expert piloting skills.

Why was I afraid of this? This is great!

Before reaching its next target, Neil's drone began to wobble. He fidgeted with the controls, but the rotor blades began to spin even faster.

Phoomp! Phoomp!

Like a T-shirt cannon at a basketball game, Neil's robot began firing projectile baked goods into the audience. Scone after scone peppered the crowd.

Uh-oh.

Neil tried to steer his robot back toward the stage, but it wasn't responding. He panicked and mashed every button available, but nothing worked. He turned off the power switch on the back, but the drone kept flying. It spun in chaotic loops, unloading its supply of scones.

"That's gonna leave a bruise!" yelled a man in an orange T-shirt, rubbing the top of his bald head. Neil heard someone laugh from backstage and glanced in that direction.

He could only see a girl's profile, as her face was covered in shadows, and frizzy hair. She laughed once more, a nasal cackle.

"Land that thing, kid!" hollered a voice. Neil turned back to the audience and saw that the robot had gone haywire.

He tried to maneuver the robot toward the ground, but he couldn't control it. It was overheating, and a chocolate scone was turning into a gooey mess. Molten chocolate leaked out from the bottom. People began to duck under their seats.

"Neil, your robot is pooping!" yelled Janey.

Neil's face went red.

"Sorry, everyone. This isn't normally how this goes,"

he shouted, his voice cracking.

From the side of the stage, Ameer appeared. Marla was with him, her robot poodle in her hands.

Woof! Woof!

With the poodle's high-pitched bark, Neil's robot quickly turned off, falling onto the lap of a stranger. The poodle's radio frequency had scrambled all the electronics in Neil's drone.

"Wow, that's some bark!" Ameer shouted. "It looks like we might have our champion!"

Ameer proudly raised Marla's hand as Neil watched an angry group of people pull raisins out of their hair.

"Better luck next year, kid," said the tournament emcee. "Or, you know, maybe not. . . ."

Neil trudged down into the audience to collect his drone, knowing he'd just ruined his only chance at meeting his hero.

CHAPTER 2

NEIL ANDERTOL WOKE UP SNEEZING.

He plucked a clump of cat fur from his lips and rubbed his blurry eyes. Every night since the robotics tournament last month, he'd been reliving the fiasco in his dreams. A night spent in his friend Biggs's basement was no different—his drone disaster haunted him like a stomachache. But Neil shook off his nightmare and promised himself that today would be different. It was a day that he'd been looking forward to for weeks. After many months apart, all eleven of Neil's friends were finally back under one roof for one weekend.

"Easy with the claws, Virginia," said Neil to one of Biggs's thirteen cats. She ignored him and kept batting at his sleeping bag. Sunlight sneaked in through a tiny window near the ceiling. Biggs's house was a sun-bleached two-story, right near an ocean cove. Neil spit out cat fur and watched the squadron of cats wind through the row of barely awake kids.

These kids were some of the best video gamers in the world, and Neil's closest friends—the US government had recruited them all for top secret missions.

The two girls on their team, Sam and Corinne, were upstairs, enjoying a slumber party with Biggs's mom. Ms. Hurbigg had a telescope that was taller than Neil, so Sam was excited to stay up late and look at constellations. Neil figured Corinne was spelling the long, complicated names of distant star systems.

"Biggs, tell Connecticut to stop hissing at me," said Jason 2 from his sleeping bag. He wore a faded yellow T-shirt that read SUPER JASON in cursive.

"That's not Connecticut—that's Pennsylvania," Biggs replied. "That one with the spots on her paws is Connecticut."

"I think they all have spots on their paws," said JP, wrestling his glasses away from a brown-and-white tabby.

"Yeah, probably," Biggs said, waving a hand to shoo his cats toward the stairway.

"Biggs, how many more cats are you planning on getting? Are you going for the full fifty states?" asked JP, putting on his smudged glasses. He'd passed out while working on calculations for his science-fair project. His sleeping bag was covered in small magnets and spiraling blue wires.

"We'll see," Biggs replied, crawling out of his sleeping bag like a lanky caterpillar. He'd really shot up in the few months since he and Neil had saved the solar system, and now he was even taller.

"Or maybe I'll name a cat after my hero—Neil Andertol," joked Biggs.

"Sir Neil Andertol, the one and *only*," said Riley in his signature Renaissance-fair accent. "The fairest video gamer on Earth, and not to mention the top flight pilot and space astronaut."

"OK, OK, we get it," said Neil, blushing.

"And don't forget sleep talker," said Waffles, the Montana native and lasso enthusiast.

"He makes a good point, Neil," said Waffle's twin brother, Dale. "Pretty sure last night you mumbled something about a 'traveling pirate circus.'"

"Wait, that's in town?" said Yuri. "What are we doing going to that gaming convention?"

"And the title of best gamer on the planet is still up for debate," said Trevor. Even after a long flight from Boston to California, he was still eager to pick fights. But Neil, who had organized the weekend, was glad to see him anyway.

After Neil's embarrassing robo demonstration, his parents had promised they'd make it up to him and offered to send Neil to Reboot Robiskie's convention. Neil was going to stay at Biggs's, but he had invited his ten other counterparts along for the adventure. Through some sort of miracle, they were all able to join.

"It's not ten yet, right?" said Waffles, folding up his camouflaged bedroll. "We can't be late for the convention."

"'Tis only half past eight," said Riley, looking at the watch on his pudgy arm. He smelled vaguely like hay bales. "And I agree, we mustn't be late for Sir Reboot's World's Fair."

"It's just called RebootCon," said Neil.

"And what exactly goes on at such a convention?" asked Yuri. "I've never been. Most of the live-action role-playing I go to meets in the woods."

"RebootCon is special. There are row after row of video games you've never even seen before," said Jason 1.

"Even though this is only the third convention, I heard Reboot's flying in the highest-paid professional gamers from all over: Russia. South Korea. *Des Moines*," said Waffles.

"They have screens that are so large, they're illegal in certain countries," added JP. He carefully tucked his science project into a sturdy plastic case.

"Yuri, you'll love it. Each one gets better," explained Dale.

"Last year, they had a competition over who could play video games the longest without blinking," added his brother, Waffles. "A kid played for three hours straight, misting his eyeballs with a squirt gun."

"Well, what are we waiting for? Let's get to this Reboot conference," said Yuri excitedly.

"It's RebootCon . . . ," Neil said.

Neil and a few others began to pick up the half-eaten

bags of chips and pretzels that surrounded Biggs's television. A cat, maybe Vermont, scratched at a plate of cookies covered in plastic wrap.

"Let's get a move on, sleepyheads" came a voice from the top of the stairs.

"Rise and shine!" It was Samantha Gonzales, Neil's best friend. She flicked on the fluorescent lights in Biggs's basement.

"We've risen! Now turn those off!" yelled a squinting Jason 1. His pillow was in the shape of a football, and he used the cushion to shield his eyes.

"I'll believe it when I see it. Now get up here," Sam said.

Blatttttt.

From the front yard came the blast of a truck horn and the diesel roar of a huge engine.

"What's going on?" asked a confused Biggs. "Is this one of those home makeover shows? They've been getting my emails!"

Neil smiled, his eyes bright. "It's actually a surprise."

Neil sprinted up the stairs and out to the front yard. He rounded the corner to see a giant vehicle, its windows tinted jet black. It looked like a giant party bus. The glow of bouncing neon lights was visible through the windows. The bus had pulled into the driveway diagonally, crushing Biggs's mom's flower beds.

"Did you miss me?" asked a voice as the door swung open.

"Harris!" yelled Trevor. The rest of the group gathered in front of the rumbling vehicle.

It was Harris Beed—former evil villain, current video-game designer, and the heir to his family's Beed Industries fortune. His quick thinking was also responsible for helping Neil's team find a stolen spaceship on their last mission.

"Nah, we didn't miss you," joked Sam. "And neither did those rosebushes."

She pointed to the thorny plants crushed under the bus's thick tires.

"Oh," said Harris. "They'll be fine—let's get on the road!"

"You're here early!" said Neil. He and his friends were still in pajamas, their hair matted into bed head.

"I've got some fires to put out before the convention starts. All the ostriches for Feather Duster 3 keep yelling Taylor Swift lyrics," Harris said. "The work of a game designer is never done. Now go get dressed."

"Do we need to bring anything else?" asked Sam.

"Where we're going we don't need anything else," Harris said with a wave. "We've got sparkling energy drinks, free T-shirts from my dad, and, like, four hundred donut holes."

"Are you kids sure you don't need a ride? I'm happy to drive," said Biggs's mom, joining everyone out front.

"It's my treat, honest," said Harris. He lifted his sunglasses to survey the shrubs he'd just run over. "And my father knows a killer landscape guy. We'll get this fixed right up."

"Groovy. We'll figure it out," said Biggs's mom. She had frizzy blond hair and the same smile as her son. "And don't forget your tickets!"

She handed Neil a sealed yellow envelope.

"OK, we gotta move it, folks. Games won't deglitch themselves."

Waffles gave a loud yip and rushed to the idling bus.

"Sweet surprise, Neil," said Dale, slapping Neil's shoulder as he chased after his brother.

Neil ran back inside to throw on his favorite pair of old corduroy pants. He double-knotted the laces of a pair of old sneakers and ran back outside.

Once everyone was dressed and on board, the donut feeding frenzy began. The bus rumbled into gear, and the mirrored walls of the interior filled with blue twinkling lights.

"To RebootCon!" shouted Harris, pushing play on a speaker system that was louder than seven jet engines. Thirteen cheers went up as Neil and his best friends headed toward the highway and the famous Reboot Robiskie.

CHAPTER

3

THE PARTY BUS SKIDDED TO A STOP IN FRONT OF THE CHAOTIC San Diego convention center. Costumed gamers moved around the vehicle like a swarm of ants.

"Thanks, Vinny!" yelled Sam to the driver. She gave him a powerful high five and skipped outside.

"Just call me when you guys are done. With traffic being so bad, I'm gonna hang around here. Might go sneak around that new ketchup plant that's opening up," said the driver. "I hear they need delivery drivers. Maybe I'll check out an aquarium or something, too."

"Those things are awful, Vinny," said Biggs.

"Could you imagine being stuck in a fish tank like that? It's like if somebody made you drive around the parking lot forever," added Sam.

"I guess I never thought of it that way," said the driver, scratching the top of his round head. He pulled a card from his shirt pocket. "Just give me a ring when you're ready to head home. I'll be around. Party on."

The bus pulled away and the group clustered together in the middle of all the zombies, vampires, overdressed Vikings, and underdressed elves.

"Oh, no. Are costumes mandatory?" asked Corinne.

"I've got enough superhero costumes for eight of us," said Jason 2. "They're a little wrinkly, though. They're stuffed in my backpack."

"When was the last time you washed those?" asked Sam.

Neil cleared his throat to get the group's attention and led them toward the huge building, only to bump into the thick, steel-toed boot of a security guard.

"Registration, please," said the short guard, who had a stubbly gray-and-black beard. He was bald, but the rest of him was very hairy and covered in tattoos that resembled barbed wire.

"Registration?" said Neil.

"Yeah, kid. Or your tickets. Lemme see 'em."

Neil slid a finger under the flap of the yellow envelope containing their tickets. With a smile he reached inside and handed the stack of tickets to the security guard.

"This is a joke, right?"

Neil looked down at what he'd handed over. It was a stack of twelve seed packages. There were sunflowers, poppies, even a few forget-me-nots—but not a single ticket.

"Oh, no, Mom must have switched up the envelopes," Biggs said. He looked through the tiny packages containing an entire garden's seeds.

Neil felt a bead of sweat build on the top of his forehead. The guard impatiently cracked his knuckles.

"We've got some good seeds in here, sir," said Biggs. "These probably equal the price of the tickets."

The guard grimaced, flexing the muscles of his unusually huge jaw.

"Wait—I thought Harris said we didn't need anything?" asked Sam.

"Perhaps this is all you need," said Harris, stepping out from the back of the group. He pulled a glossy pass from his pocket and handed it to the man. The pass was stamped with the official RebootCon logo and the letters *VIP.*

VIP! Perfect. Since Harris designs games, he can totally get us all in. Neil felt a wave of relief.

"That gets you in, chief. But your friends aren't VIPs," said the guard.

Well, awesome.

Harris turned to Neil as his phone erupted with a panicked, all-caps text message. THE GLITCH IS MUTATING. NEED HELP ASAP.

"I just have my pass, guys," Harris said. "I'm sorry, but I really need to get in there. Once I fix my game, I'll try and get twelve more passes."

He scribbled a number on a Beed Industries card. "Here's the number of my booth, if you guys get inside." With that, the blue-velvet rope was secured back in place, and Harris disappeared into the stream of gamers.

"Well, OK," Neil said, sighing. He turned to the scruffy guard. "Can we use RebootCoins from the hosting site?"

"Kid, I don't even know what anything you just said means," he replied. "To get in here, you need to either be on this list of preregistered guests or have a ticket—and tickets have been sold out for days."

Neil's sweats got worse, and he instantly regretted the nineteen donut holes he'd eaten on the ride in. He couldn't be mad at Biggs's mom for the ticket oversight, but Neil was panicked.

"So let me get this straight," said Trevor. "We flew all the way across the country for a convention we don't have tickets to?"

He too had had a growth spurt since Neil saw him last. He was nearly as tall as Biggs, and his voice was getting deeper.

"Kids, you either have tickets or not. And I need this area clear. Lots of customers with *real tickets* need to get through."

Neil felt dizzy. He had worked so hard to make this trip happen, and the twelve best video gamers in the country were stuck outside the biggest video-game convention in history.

"We could try and drive back home," offered Biggs.

"With that traffic? By the time we get back, the convention will be over," said Trevor. He put his hands on his hips and huffed out in frustration. "Why wasn't I put in charge of this? We wouldn't be in this mess if I was the one responsible."

The group shuffled away from the entrance.

"Sorry about the seeds, everybody. We tried," Biggs said. "We can still have a good time. My mom can make us beet pancakes at home."

The group groaned. They wanted a chance to see the mysterious Reboot Robiskie, not to introduce more fiber into their diets.

"It's OK. It's nobody's fault," said Neil.

"Man, I was really looking forward to this convention," said Yuri.

"I know," said Waffles. "And now we're stuck here with nothing to do. I could be playing paintball right now."

"I should be finishing my science project!" said a stressed JP.

"Guys, I—I don't know what to say, but—" Neil started.

"Save it for another time, Andertol," said Sam, her eyes scanning the crowd. "I think I've got an idea."

★ ★ ★

TEN MINUTES LATER. AT THE OPPOSITE END OF THE building—at a completely separate entrance—a group of twelve arrived in an elegant party bus. Its pulsing neon lights were turned off, and soft classical music played inside.

Sam was the first to leave the bus, again, as Neil and the others silently followed.

"Tell everyone Mr. Beed sends his regards," said Vinny, the bus driver, in a fake British accent.

Everyone wore baggy, neon-green shirts plastered with the logo of Beed Industries.

"Tickets, please," asked a different security guard. She was taller than the first and wore a black baseball cap with the official RebootCon insignia.

"What for? We'll be in and out—just here to help behind the scenes," Sam said, her usually gruff voice seeming the tiniest bit raspier. "Booth three hundred and thirty."

She handed over Harris's card. It was very thick paper, and the guard ran her fingers over the grooves of Harris Beed's family insignia.

"What is it you all are doing exactly?"

"Fixing the booth for Feather Duster 3. The game keeps glitching."

The woman looked puzzled. "Beed Industries?"

"You don't know Beed Industries?" Sam asked. "Lady, they're the main sponsors of RebootCon." She pointed up at the show's banner; it read REBOOTCON: PROUDLY SPONSORED BY BEED INDUSTRIES.

"There's no time to waste. If we don't get in to fix his game, we're all in trouble," Sam said. "*Especially* anyone responsible for keeping us from fixing Mr. Beed's game."

Sam made a pretty convincing negotiator. The guard inspected the card once again, then studied the group's T-shirts, and finally looked back at the banner.

"We'll be in and out, promise," Sam said.

"Fine, just be quick about it," she replied. The guard unclipped the blue rope and waved the twelve fake Beed Industries employees into the convention center. Neil Andertol smiled, proud of Sam's quick thinking. *RebootCon. We did it. We're in.*

CHAPTER

4

"THIS . . . IS REBOOTCON." A VOICE THUNDERED THROUGH hidden speakers that lined the long, tunnellike hallway that led to the main floor.

"Why is it so dark in this place?" asked Corinne.

Fake fog began to ooze across the floor, and the tunnel began to widen. The group kept walking through the bluish haze.

Roaarrr!

A giant shark swooped down from the ceiling, its jaws opened wide. The beast had huge, sinister eyes and was headed straight toward Neil.

"Flying sharks! It's finally happening!" screamed Biggs, tucking his head and arms inside his XXL Beed Industries T-shirt.

"Relax, weirdo, it's just a hologram," said Trevor.

Neil looked at the shark and saw that Trevor was actually right—it was a hologram, and an incredibly lifelike one at that. As the shark swam away, the same voice boomed again.

"Be the first to play the never-before-seen Captain Jolly's Shark Hunt. Only at RebootCon."

Cool, a brand-new game.

They finally entered the convention center, a genuine gaming paradise, full of everything Neil had dreamed of. The maze of booths contained game prototypes and lots of free swag—from coffee cups to sunglasses. Crazed convention-goers ran from one booth to the next, arms full of goodies.

"Dudes, there's a game about tying knots for speed," said Dale. "This is the best day of my life."

"And, my heavens, a game about saddle oiling!" Riley cried.

Practically all the games were new, with a few using

some of the latest motion-capture technology. One offered the most realistic sled-riding simulation, while others re-created ancient battles.

"Hey! How'd you guys get in?" said Harris. Neil looked around but couldn't see his friend.

"Harris!" Neil said, a little surprised. "Harris?"

"Down here," said his voice. He was sitting on the floor, repairing his game's console. It was a retro stand-up arcade game, like the one Neil had played at the pizza parlor. A few kids in Feather Duster 3 outfits were manning the booth. Neil glanced up to see he was in front of booth 330.

"I'm glad you guys made it in," said Harris, half his attention still on his malfunctioning game.

"Us too," replied Trevor.

"This place is pretty cool, right? My employees said that Reboot might come into the building—I can't believe it," said Harris. "Pretty risky move. He's wanted by, like, five different countries for not taking down his website."

Neil could hear the eagerness in Harris's voice. International gaming fugitives could turn even Harris into a fanboy.

"Hey, JP, mind taking a look at this with me?" asked

Harris. "I could use any help I can get. I'm getting error messages I've never even encountered before."

As JP and the others crowded around Harris and his ostrich arcade game, Neil's, Sam's, and Biggs's attention was drawn to the back of the room.

Along the wall was a big stage with a huge screen in the shape of a hundred-foot shark. In front, black curtains covered two bulky objects the size of bulldozers.

"RebootCon! Are you ready?" announced a voice through the speakers.

"What is that game?" asked Neil in a trance. "What's going on?"

"Oh, that? Another world premiere," said one of Harris's assistants. She wore the same Beed Industries T-shirt as Neil but also sported an ostrich-beak nose. "Captain Jolly's Shark Hunt. It's from a new designer; nobody really knows anything about it. Looks pretty cutting-edge, though."

"Sharks, really?" Neil questioned. "I mean, they're cool—I just need something faster."

"Oh, it's plenty fast. So powerful it takes three people to control it."

"Oh, whoa, three people? That sounds intense."

"It's supposed to be the best game here."

Neil looked toward the stage and began pushing through the crowd. The new game pulled him like a magnet. He had to play it. Lately, Neil had been desperate for a new game. He had been breaking all his high scores, whether it was controlling jets, ostriches, or spacecraft. Not from a cheat code, but from Neil being too good, apparently. It was as if the games were letting him know he needed a new challenge.

"And looks like you'll be playing second, ManofNeil," said Sam, edging a few steps ahead of Neil. She happened to be a big fan of sharks. Neil went faster, breaking into a run—his first exercise since last week's gym class.

"And I call dibs on third!" said Biggs, his frame bobbing with long strides.

The trio dodged a small army of ax-wielding goblins before arriving at the huge shark-shaped screen. They watched a girl in a shark costume grab hold of the black curtains hiding the two giant objects.

"People of RebootCon. I'm Miss Jolly Rogers the Third. And behold, Captain Jolly's Shark Hunt," announced the girl. The stage and convention center went dark as she pulled back the curtains.

The spotlights revealed two monstrous shark heads. Each had room for three players to stand in its open jaws and view the screen through the foot-long teeth.

"Ladies and gentlemen," she said, "I'm your host, referee, and commentator, here to take you all on the hunt."

She wore a headset microphone, and her long hair was a dark crimson that framed her slender face. It was dotted with tiny freckles, making her skin look like sunburned porcelain.

In a foam shark costume, she walked the stage confidently, giving the crowd a big smile. She strutted like a runway model.

"Who dares to brave the sting of defeat for a chance at fame?"

Neil stepped closer to the stage.

"We dare!" shouted Biggs, waving his hands. "We will dare that sting!"

"Well then, step right up!" answered Jolly.

"Wait, but how do you play?" asked Neil.

"Who knows!" said Biggs.

He took the stage with a giant leap, while Neil and Sam took the stairs. They met up in one of the fake shark heads. It was incredibly lifelike, and Neil had to touch its skin to make sure it wasn't actually slimy and wet.

"Is this supposed to be a megalodon?" asked Sam. She studied the fake teeth intensely.

"Indeed," said Jolly. "The fiercest, most gigantic pre-historic shark that ever existed. The most powerful sea creature there ever was."

"Even compared to those mythical squids?" said Biggs.

"Biggs, if the megalodon were still alive today, every single creature would be in trouble," said Sam. "It probably would've evolved, grown legs, and eaten all of us. These sharks had hundreds of giant teeth, each up to seven inches long!"

"Be warned, Beed family," continued Jolly. "This will not be easy."

"We're definitely not a family!" corrected Sam.

"Well, you're all snazzy dressers, that's for sure," the host said. "And, facing off in the megalodon jaws across from you, your opponents."

Jolly welcomed three young ladies dressed as mermaids who would pilot the other shark.

"Now—battle stations, everyone!"

Neil, Biggs, and Sam shuffled to the three control podiums. Neil was in the center, with Sam to his right.

"Before we get started, enter your names from Reboot's site to pull up your profiles," said Jolly. "We want to keep any records set here today."

Neil looked out to the crowd that had formed. So many people were watching, and he tried to forget the fiasco that had happened with his drone.

"My, my," said Jolly as Neil, Biggs, and Sam tapped in their screen names. Their high scores for games hosted on Reboot Robiskie's server popped up. "You lot are very impressive. Take your positions."

The lights on the stage dimmed as a countdown from twenty seconds began. Neil clasped his hands together to stretch his fingers.

16 . . . 15 . . . 14 . . .

"I call next game," shouted Trevor. "I'll show you all how it's done."

"This match is a timed event, and winners will receive a free copy of the game as well as a lifetime supply of Rogers ketchup, the main sponsor of Captain Jolly's Shark Hunt!" said Jolly, raising her hands to drum up applause. She had the endless energy of an infomercial salesperson. "Throughout the level, there are gold coins in a pirate shipwreck. Steer your shark to collect the gold. The team that collects the most coins and deposits them back at their team treasure chest wins."

9 . . . 8 . . . 7 . . .

Neil surveyed the game. The level was a rocky underwater scene, with glimmering coins buried in groves of seaweed and coral cliffs.

"And one more thing," said Jolly. She pushed a button on her tiny control console, and two massive holograms of the sharks appeared over the audience. The sharks swam in place with realistic fin movements as gold coins twirled overhead. It was like the stage, and the entire convention center, was one huge video game.

3 . . . 2 . . . 1

In a flurry of bubbles, Neil's shark quickly began to cruise through the level. Biggs was in charge of the tail fin, which controlled the speed. Using a motion-sensing control, Biggs waved his arms to help their shark accelerate.

"Prepare to watch the most graceful tail wagging you've ever seen," said Biggs.

Sam was in charge of biting, diving, and surfacing, and Neil steered. After logging countless flight hours together, both real and in virtual reality, the three worked well as a team.

Their hologram shark swam through the game's level, chomping down gold coins. Neil steered them back toward the team's treasure chest to deposit their haul. Sam had the shark dive low, skimming just above the outstretched hands of convention attendees.

"Thirty seconds left!" said Jolly, turning to the audience. "Let's see if the Beeds can pull it off! Cheer them on, RebootCon!"

Neil glanced backward to see more and more gamers crowding around to watch. He and his friends, in the span of twenty minutes, had become the most exciting part of RebootCon.

Neil saw the rest of his crew in front of the stage, screaming as if he and their friends were headlining a sold-out rock concert.

"I see you've got some fellow family members cheering you on from the crowd," said Jolly. "Wow, quite a few. Well, aren't you lucky."

As Neil steered toward a coin just past a pillar of coral, a huge set of jaws chomped at him from above.

"Whoa!" Neil yelled.

"No fair—they have to go for the coins," said Biggs.

"I don't recall that being in the rules," said Jolly. "Fifteen seconds left!"

The crowd pushed up against the stage, frenzied for the final few seconds. The mermaids were playing dirty, but Neil had made quick work of gathering most of the gold. Only five gold coins remained on the level.

"Let's go, Neil," said Sam. "Show all these gamers how to do it!"

Sam and Neil steered the shark down through strands of seaweed and schools of yellow fish, speeding toward each spinning piece of pirate treasure. They effortlessly collected the final coins, dodging the ferocious bites from the mermaids' shark.

"Winners!" shouted Jolly as hologram ocean confetti burst out over the energetic crowd. Neil watched his shark opponent sink, its glowing red eyes disappearing into murky blue-green water.

Jolly quickly ushered the mermaids offstage, careful not to step on their tails.

"Well, well, the Beed family stays alive," said Jolly. "Who will be next?"

Hands raised in all corners of the convention center.

"Me! Me!" screamed Trevor. The host cupped a hand to her ear, egging the crowd on. With a devilish smile she walked to the other side of the stage.

Jolly pointed to a clawed hand in the crowd, and Neil watched three gargoyles take the set of jaws across from him. Once again, on Jolly's mark, the ancient sharks were back at it, twirling through the ocean and over thousands of people. Neil was soon trying tricky maneuvers to gain speed while cruising underwater valleys. He was getting the hang of steering, and Biggs was working up a sweat flinging his body to speed them along.

Round after round passed with Neil, Sam, and Biggs as victors. The gargoyles were quickly defeated and were followed by knights. The knights fought hard but then gave way to the vampires, who sucked.

Neil and his friends battled through six more groups of costumed convention-goers, honing their skills with each match. The talkative Jolly went quiet during their matches.

Suddenly, in the middle of a match against a feisty trio of frost giants, the game paused.

Neil's controls stopped working, and he looked back to see a bunch of security guards surrounding his friends. A guard climbed onto the stage and whispered something into Jolly's ear.

"Hey, no pushing!" yelled Waffles from below the stage.

"Well, this may mean a disqualification," Jolly said, shaking her head. "Apparently, some of our players snuck into the conference."

"ManofNeil, run!" yelled Jason 2. "Save those precious gaming hands of yours!"

Neil's crew was surrounded, and the guards began to herd them back toward the entrance.

"Hey, easy with my friends!" Neil yelled as a female guard began to corner Dale and Waffles. It was the one who'd allowed them inside the convention, and she grabbed the brothers by their shirt collars.

"Beed Industries, eh? Bet you thought you were pretty smart," the guard said to them. "You're coming with me."

"Does this mean I don't get to play? Are you kidding me?" Trevor whined.

A guard almost had Neil's hands pinned behind his back when Jolly Rogers stepped in.

"Let these three come with me," she said. Her eyes

sparkled. "I'll make sure our cheaters still get a free copy of the game, then have them removed from the premises."

Neil could feel Jolly's thin fingers wrap around his wrist. She squeezed tightly, making sure he couldn't wriggle free from her grip. She *really* wanted him to have that game.

"Radio me after," said the guard. She ducked under the stage to go after Yuri. He'd crawled below the metal stage, but he didn't get far before getting tangled in a mess of lighting cords.

As Yuri was dragged out by his foot, a kid in a white nautical uniform stepped between Neil and Jolly. He was nearly as tall as the girl, and the two towered over Neil.

"You're not taking them anywhere," said the teen-ager. He wore a black-brimmed white captain's hat, with a silver *R* embroidered on its front.

He spoke with a calm voice that reminded Neil of Weo, a friend he'd made when he'd crash-landed a jet into his island tree house.

"He wants to see him," said the teen.

He?

"And who is 'he'?" said Jolly. Her smile was long gone.

"You don't know?" the teen said. "*He* is the man of the hour—Reboot Robiskie. And he wants to see these three."

Wait, Reboot Robiskie asked to see us? No way.

"Well, we can't go anywhere without our friends," said Sam. "If Reboot wants to see us, we go as a team."

The boy looked at Sam in surprise. It was like she'd passed on the chance to meet royalty.

"I'm afraid that's not how this works," he said. "I can't help your friends. Mr. Robiskie *only* wants to see the three gamers who just played."

"But *I* need to see the three gamers who just played," Jolly said. Her voice had completely lost its warmth.

"Can I kick these kids out or what?" yelled the impatient security guard, who was nearly done collecting the rest of Neil's group. She had Jason 2 trapped in his cape, and another security official chased down Trevor as he tried to play Captain Jolly's Shark Hunt.

Neil was uncertain what to do. Both the creator of an awesome new game and, apparently, Reboot Robiskie wanted to see him and his friends.

"It's now or never," said the boy in the white outfit.

"Neil, you guys have got to go see Reboot," said Waffles. "For me! For all of us!"

Neil looked at Sam, then Biggs.

"Listen to my brother! Save yourselves!" shouted Dale. "We'll get a ride back in Harris's donut bus!"

The three onstage nodded, and Neil grabbed the shoulder of the sharply dressed boy.

"Sorry, Jolly. Loved your game, though."

Neil felt her let go of his wrist as he was led off the stage and through a secret exit of the convention center. As Neil pushed through a heavy door, he looked back to see Jolly returning to the lights of the stage, her game demonstration still happening.

"Who needs them anyway, right?" Jolly shouted to the crowd. "On to my next victims!"

CHAPTER 5

OK. THAT WAS A LEFT. ANOTHER LEFT. AND TWO RIGHTS.

Neil, Biggs, and Sam were led through the winding corridors below the main level of the convention center. Neil did his best to remember their route, just in case something happened. From years of video gaming, Neil never entered a room without remembering how to find his way back out.

"You guys doin' OK?" Neil turned and asked the two friends behind him. They nodded.

"I do feel bad leaving everybody like that," said Sam.

"Me, too, but they understand," Neil answered. "They'd do the same thing if they were in our shoes."

"Well, it's too late to turn back now," said Biggs, looking at a message on his phone. "JP says they're already outside. He says they'll figure something out for a couple hours."

"I guess so . . . ," Sam replied.

"Yeah, they're fine," Biggs said. "I'm sending them my mom's number. She'll have beet pancakes ready for their return."

Blech. Let's not return.

They continued to follow the kid in uniform. "Sorry there's not room for everyone," he said. "We only allow a few people on the yacht at a time."

Yacht? We get to go on Reboot's yacht?!

"I'm the same way about my yacht," Neil joked, trying to downplay his excitement.

The boy did not laugh.

"I mean, thank you, this is an honor," Neil said. He knew that Reboot lived in international waters so authorities could never successfully shut down his operation, but he never thought he'd ever see his hero's home base. Neil wondered if it would live up to the messy standards of his own room back home.

The group walked down a final hallway before pushing through double doors and into the bright sunlight. They were near the industrial shipping dock for the convention center. Sunshine sparkled across the ocean marina.

Neil was ushered onto a ladder on the water's edge and looked down. The sea was a few feet below. An inflatable raft with a small motor was waiting at the bottom of a few rusted metal rungs.

"Wait, is this the yacht? 'Cause if so I'm going back," said Sam.

"Ha, good one," said the boy, sliding down the ladder. "I'm Wifi, by the way. Just hop aboard. You won't regret it."

Sam hopped down the rungs, and the raft dipped as her feet landed firmly. Neil and Biggs followed, and Wifi untied the raft from the dock. The engine revved, and they cruised out of the marina and into the open ocean.

This is either the best or worst idea we've ever had.

Neil's body slammed into the bottom of the raft as it bounced over choppy waves. His stomach did its best to keep up with the raft as the coastline slowly faded away.

A BIT WOBBLY, NEIL STEPPED ONTO THE SHINY WHITE DECK of a forty-foot yacht. Neil glanced in every direction and saw nothing but miles of ocean.

Wow, we're far out. This view is a bit different from Colorado.

The ship had two levels and some pretty sophisticated-looking equipment spinning around on the roof. Neil figured it was some kind of cloaking device—Reboot was a wanted man, after all.

The lower deck, decorated with white leather couches that were comically large, led into a massive kitchen. It looked like there was enough room for twenty-five people. Neil counted four different refrigerators.

"You could throw an ultimate party on here. You sure we can't bring our friends?" asked Neil. The teen didn't respond.

"Up top," called a voice from the higher deck of the ship.

Neil looked at Sam, whose eyes were wide.

"This is like meeting Sasquatch, guys," Biggs said, doing his best to tame his unruly long hair.

At the top, a large white leather chair was perched in

front of a bay of screens. Some displayed spiking charts and graphs, while others showed video feeds. One screen looked like the feed from Captain Jolly's Shark Hunt.

"Welcome," said a voice from behind the high back of the captain's chair. The chair turned with a squeak to reveal a boy in sunglasses. He had light-brown skin and wore white pants and a half-buttoned shirt. He sipped a frozen drink through a curly-q straw. "Reboot Robiskie is the name."

Uh, dude, we know. I just didn't think you were the same age as me.

"I'm Biggs, and this is Sam Gonzales and Neil. Neil Andertol."

The boy noisily slurped from his drink.

"You may know me from my work with smellable gaming," continued Biggs. "Or the Universal Biggs Language—which is now a legally recognized language in almost two different states *and* Nova Scotia." Sam nudged him to stop talking.

"All of you were impressive in the convention," the kid hacker said. "Especially you, Neil."

"You're right—he's the best gamer alive," Sam said.

"Your voice is familiar," said Reboot, looking at Sam.

"We've flown jets together, haven't we?"

"Wait, you just play regular games?" asked a shocked Neil.

"From time to time. I like to keep the skills sharp," Reboot said. "ShooterSam, I take it."

Sam nodded.

"I see you've met Wifi Whitner," he said, gesturing to the teen. "He's my right-hand man and only crewmate. There's not a glitch, motor malfunction, or bug he can't fix."

Wifi nodded. Neil's eyes turned back to Reboot.

"Frozen smoothie, anyone?" asked Reboot Robiskie. "We collect the rarest and tastiest fruit around the world to make them—they're great."

"Yes, please!" said Neil. *Now this is the life.*

Wifi disappeared downstairs and soon returned with a tray full of frosty glasses containing red and blue slush. Neil was already loving his time at sea, and he wondered if it was too soon to ask for an all-white uniform so that he'd look like a real sea captain.

A smoothie was handed to Reboot, and he stood up from his chair to propose a toast. The five raised their glasses together.

- -

"To you three," Reboot said with a grin. "Well done today."

"I'll cheers to that. To the best friends ever!" said Neil.

The five took long sips of the sugary frozen drink. Neil didn't even care that he got a brain freeze. He knew the moment would be etched forever in his memory, once his brain thawed.

Biggs released his curly straw from his mouth and raised his glass again.

"And another toast—to Reboot Robiskie," said Biggs. "And his boat full of video games and great-tasting frozen treats."

As Neil finished his tropical fruit smoothie, another instantly replaced it, with what seemed like an even bigger, crazier straw.

"So are you not allowed into your own convention?" asked Sam. "Isn't it weird to not be there?"

"I wish I could be there, but if I set foot on land, I'll get arrested. Plus I don't like crowds," Reboot said. "When I want, I bring the best part of the convention to me."

"Are you talking about those futuristic hand dryers in the bathrooms? They seemed pretty hard to move," said Biggs. He was leaning on the ship's railing as he looked toward the setting sun.

"I think he means us, dude," said Neil. "And thanks. That Shark Hunt game was fun. Why don't you have it on the site yet?"

"I didn't know it existed until a couple days ago," Reboot said. "A copy showed up unannounced. I played it once and was hooked—let the creator know I'd save the convention space if they wanted to debut the game."

"Who's the creator?" asked Neil.

"Not too sure. I've found in this business some things need to be kept secret, Neil," said Reboot. He pushed his sunglasses to the top of his head. "But if you guys are interested in stuff like that, want to see the server room?"

"You bet we do," said Neil.

You bet we do? You're hanging out with the most wanted hacker in the world, you're not allowed to talk like your goofy uncle. Get it together, Neil Andertol.

Neil, Sam, and Biggs followed Reboot Robiskie inside, past the fancy kitchen. They reached a large white door, and Reboot tapped in a lengthy code. The door clicked open.

They entered a small room inside the nose of the ship. A wall of gigantic television screens displayed streaming videos from gamers currently in battle. In the corner of each TV was the country and time zone of the game's origin. From a black metal tower in the corner, the site's server hummed.

Neil watched kids in India face off in a level of Chameleon. Below that was a tournament-style game of Feather Duster 2. He looked a few screens over to see someone playing Riley's favorite, Horse Jump 3. Neil felt a bit guilty.

Riley should be here to see this.

"And you control all these games?" asked Biggs.

"Not control, really," Reboot said. "But they're all hosted from the boat. I want everyone to have a place to be free to post what he or she wants," said Reboot.

"I wish my friends could see this," Neil said. "Do your friends get to hang out and play with you?"

Reboot paused and took a second to finish his last gulp of smoothie.

"Believe it or not, it's hard to have friends when you live on a boat," Reboot said. Sam gave Reboot a pat on the shoulder.

"Hey, guys . . . not to get sidetracked, but are you hungry?" asked Biggs, his stomach gurgling with hunger.

"We missed all the concession stands while playing that shark game."

"Megalodon," Sam corrected.

"Yeah, and what exactly is that?" said Biggs. "In front of the creator, I was playing it cool, but I still feel like 'megalodon' is a type of haircut."

"Megalodons were almost like huge dinosaurs of the sea and lived about ten million years ago. Think sharks but ten times bigger. Apex predators," said Reboot. "They ruled the seas during an age far more dangerous than our own."

"Righteous," said Biggs.

"But to answer your food question, we can make whatever you want," Reboot said.

"Our weight in mozzarella sticks?" asked Biggs.

"Hmm. That's a new one," said Reboot, rubbing his chin. "How about pizza? What kind do you like?"

"Pineapple!" the three said in unison, remembering their favorite pie from Penny's Island Pizza.

"Well, pineapple it is," said Reboot. "Let's party."

He wandered out to the fancy kitchen and opened a freezer full of frozen pies. He unwrapped two huge pizzas as Wifi sliced up a fresh pineapple. The rest of the fridges contained an endless supply of energy drinks, juices, travel yogurts, and sodas from around the world. Their labels were in Arabic, Japanese, and Russian. Neil understood that sugar was a universal language.

"It's the most beautiful thing I've ever seen," said Sam. Neil was speechless. When the pizza was ready, Neil chowed down on slice after slice as Reboot told tales of his high-seas exploits.

"Guys, I don't want to be a buzzkill," said Biggs, his mouth full of Peruvian hot cocoa. "But we should get back soon. Everybody was going to stay at my house another night, plus I've got like ninety litter boxes to clean."

"Don't worry. I've contacted your mother on behalf of the Robiskie Foundation, letting her know the three of you were selected as convention guests of honor, receiving a free night's stay," said Wifi. "As for the cat litter, you're on your own."

"Riley will help your mom out, I'm sure," said Neil.

"Anyone care for cereal dessert?" asked Reboot. He opened boxes of exotic cereal from Panama and Vancouver. Neil ate fistfuls of sugary flakes and chocolate-flavored puffy puffs. His tongue was raw from the sugar overload, but he was in bliss. With Biggs and Sam fading, Neil and Reboot Robiskie moved to his server room to watch kids across the globe do Chameleon battle. The room glowed with the flashing of screens. A few tiny white lights were built into the ceiling.

"I could live forever on this yacht," said Neil. "And I get seasick pretty easily, so that's saying something."

Reboot chuckled.

"You all are funny. It's good to have you aboard."

For someone living every kid's dream, Reboot Robiskie didn't seem very enthusiastic. Neil imagined a life of constantly being on the run, though. It would get old fast.

"Is it just you and Wifi out here all the time? I bet you guys get bored," said Neil. "You do have space for a bigger crew."

"It's the life we've chosen," Reboot said. "And I've learned it's very hard to find people to trust."

"Why do you trust us?"

"Call it a hunch."

Neil slurped his slushie and looked at the games Reboot was currently hosting. A pleasant moment of silence passed between them.

"I like collecting things from parts of the world

people couldn't even imagine," Reboot said, the fans from his server flipping on in the background. "Like my newest toy; I call it 'The Crow's Nest.'"

Reboot pulled out a small drone from a dark corner of the room. It looked a lot like Neil's back home.

"No way! That thing is awesome."

"It *was* awesome. But I broke it last week when I was escaping from the Japanese coast guard."

"I made one for myself, but I broke it, too. . . . It went haywire at a robotics convention."

"That's still pretty cool that you made it yourself," said Reboot, placing the robot back on the ground.

He and Neil plopped into comfy chairs. It was somewhere near noon in Shanghai when Neil's eyes finally closed, his smiling lips stained purple.

CHAPTER

6

"OH, SWEET MERCIFUL FRUCTOSE," SAID NEIL, HIS EYES WHIP-
ping open. He'd fallen asleep in a chair surrounded by
video games. Neil's breath smelled like dried slugs. He
slowly got up and walked out onto the lower level of the
ship. It was morning, and the sun was just beginning
to crawl up over the horizon. Neil looked around for
Reboot, but he was nowhere to be found.

*Must be in his quarters. I wish I could live somewhere
with quarters.*

Neil did his best to clean up as he made his way

to the top deck, grabbing half-full bags of candy and picking up some of the few hundred mozzarella sticks covering the stairs.

Biggs and Sam were on either side of the top deck, both still asleep. Biggs's lips were stained purple, and Sam's glasses were covered in caramel.

"Rise and shine, recruits," Neil said. "We accidentally went into candy hibernation, I think."

"Ughhh," said Biggs, squinting in the sun.

"Yeah, I know," said Neil. "But it was worth it. Can you believe we just stayed on Reboot's yacht?"

"I think there was a Swedish Fish migration in my intestines last night," said Biggs. He'd spent the night on a white cushioned bench, using the cardboard from the frozen pizzas for a blanket.

Sam sat up from her makeshift nest of fluffy towels.

"Where's Reboot?" she asked, doing her best to comb out her bed head. "And do you have any vegetables or fruit on this ship? I think my body is in sugar shock."

Biggs examined the leftover pizza.

"We might have a few pineapple slices," he replied. "But that's about it."

The sky grew lighter above the calm ocean.

Seagulls flocked overhead, looking for snacks.

"Good morning," said Wifi. "Mr. Robiskie has arranged for you to be taken to Mr. Hurbigg's residence."

"Who's that?" asked Biggs, pulling half-eaten gummy candies from his pockets before popping them into his mouth. "Oh, right. That's me."

"Do we get to say good-bye?" asked Neil.

"Mr. Robiskie hates saying good-bye. And anyway, he can watch you any time you log onto his site. We also will be in contact about being part of our video-game selection committee. For the games we choose to host," the kid replied.

"Awesome," said Sam.

"Mr. Robiskie said to tell you that he considers you friends, and that he does anything for friends. Now let's go—your ride is ready."

★ ★ ★

NEIL. BIGGS. AND SAM JUMPED INTO SHALLOW WATER JUST off a small beach. Biggs's house was at the top of the cove.

"Thanks for the lift, Wifi," said Biggs, waving back to the boat.

They'd been given fresh, all-white outfits, but they were already soaked up to their knees. There were only size-medium outfits, so Biggs's pant legs stopped with six inches of shin left to go.

"Yuck," said Neil. He pulled his foot out of the mucky sand to find some seaweed tangled around his ankle. The smell of fish was in the air, blowing in with the strong ocean breeze. Biggs looked up toward his house.

"Well," said Biggs, gazing at his humble abode. "I wonder if they made it back last night. . . ."

"And if they did, I wonder if the cats got the best of 'em," joked Neil.

Sam gave a halfhearted laugh.

"Like Wifi said, Reboot took care of everyone," Neil reassured them.

"You guys don't feel like we ditched everybody?" she asked. She'd held her shoes in her hand, like a smart person, and was putting them back on as Neil wrung out the wet cuffs of his pants.

"I guess we kind of did, in a technical sense," Neil said. "But we just had a night on Reboot Robiskie's secret yacht, guys. You know how many kids would want that chance?"

"Thousands," said Biggs.

"Worldwide, probably millions," said Neil. "And we

got to live it. I bet everyone else had a blast playing games at Biggs's house."

"I know we're lucky. Would've just been nice to have our whole group there is all," Sam said. She started hiking uphill toward Biggs's house.

Neil tried to follow, but strong arms suddenly grabbed him from behind. For the second time in a year, Neil felt the coarse fibers of a large burlap bag being pulled over his head. It was quickly secured around his waist, and a drawstring was cinched, restricting his arms and hands.

"Gah!" he yelled.

Neil was hoisted up from the sand, his legs thrashing as if he were on an invisible bicycle. He was thrown over someone's shoulder.

"What's happening?" yelled Sam. Neil could hear panic in her voice. "Who are you?!"

"Oh, no!" screamed Biggs. "I know who it is. The recycling police!"

"What?" screamed Sam.

"I threw an aluminum can away in the regular trash at that convention," Biggs explained. "They must've got me on video. I've let Earth down!"

Neil, however, was unsure that the recycling police was

an official arm of the government. . . . It could only be . . .

Stuck in a burlap sack, Neil stopped fighting. He felt overwhelmingly calm.

"Wait, guys. I know who it is!" Neil said, smiling. "We're back to burlap bags now, Jonesy? Wanna keep the mission a secret this time?"

"Wait, you really think this is Jones?" asked Biggs.

"Of course! Who else would it be?"

"Neil, I'm not so sure. I've got a weird feeling about this," said Sam.

"Guys, trust me," Neil replied. Neil heard the sound of crashing waves grow closer as he was carried back to the ocean. "Now take us away, Jones. Let's see what you've got in store for us this time."

A loud grunt replied, and Neil was thrown from someone's broad shoulder onto a boat. Neil heard the creak of a door, and he was picked up again and brought belowdecks. Biggs was just to his right, Sam at his left. It was completely dark.

"You guys doing OK?" Neil asked.

"Well, we're in burlap bags on a boat. Not sure if 'OK' would describe what's really happening," said Sam. "But I'm alive, yes."

"Don't worry," Neil reassured her. "I'm sure Jones has another mission that needs saving—and we're the only ones to do it."

"If you say so," said Biggs. "But you have to help me with my composting if we get put in recycling jail."

"I'll be your cell mate," Neil said. "The rest of the group must be waiting for us. Jones wouldn't have known where to find us on Reboot's yacht. Nobody can find that thing by design."

With a jolt, the boat headed out to sea. Neil Andertol was excited.

"Just you wait, guys—our most amazing mission is about to start."

CHAPTER 7

AFTER TWENTY MINUTES OF LYING ON AN UNFORGIVING metal floor, Neil had lost feeling in his feet and hands. Unlike in previous kidnappings, Neil, Sam, and Biggs were lashed together, and the metal floor was cold and wet, and smelled a bit like fish guts, even through the burlap sack. It was difficult to move, and Neil had already tried to escape unsuccessfully. He was dripping sweat.

"OK, so maybe I was wrong about the mission thing," admitted Neil. "I'm starting to get a weird feeling about this—beyond seasickness, that is."

"Ya think?" said Sam. "I've been trying to get a hand free for the last twenty minutes."

"Yeah, I don't know if this is Jones," said Biggs. "Also, does anybody else smell ketchup?"

"I only smell trout guts," said Neil. "Let's work together to get these things off us so we can see where we are, at least."

"Sounds like a plan," said Sam.

"I have a couple fingers and half a foot free," said Biggs. "Maybe we can untie one another."

The three friends scrunched together. Neil could feel Sam's wrists and the fraying cord. He searched for the end of the knot.

"Do we have anything sharp to try to cut us free?" asked Neil.

"Yeah, sure thing. Let me just reach into my knife supply," Sam said sarcastically.

"It was worth a shot!" defended Neil.

"Wait, I might have something!" said Biggs. "Can anybody reach my right pocket?"

"Wait, do you seriously have a knife?" Sam asked.

"Gimme a second. I think I can reach you, Biggs," said Neil. He twisted his body. "What is this?"

"Last night Reboot gave me this candy from Singapore. It's like goo," said Biggs. "I couldn't stop eating it. I had a package and a half this morning, so I figured I'd take it with me. It's pretty much red sugar-slime."

"And I'm the one that gets to stick his hands in it? Lucky me!" said Neil.

"Listen, I've got the slender, unblemished hands of a professional hand model and we all know it," said Biggs. "I can squeeze out of these ropes. I just need a little help."

Neil rolled his eyes and stretched out his fingertips, fishing a hand into his friend's pocket. He found something in the shape of a half-used toothpaste container.

"Got it!" Neil said. He carefully plucked the candy goo from Biggs's pocket, making sure not to drop it on the wet floor. Neil passed the slimy toothpaste tube to Sam, who was able to squeeze some out onto Biggs's arms, which were tied behind his back.

Neil could feel his friend squirm.

"Almost out . . . just a few more seconds . . ."

Neil was starting to worry about the location of his other friends. *If this isn't a mission, then where is everyone else? Are they locked up somewhere, too?*

"Yes! I'm out!" said Biggs, untying the knots around Sam's hands. "Now don't waste any more of that candy goo—that's precious stuff."

Once Sam was free, the two squirmed to help Neil. He was happy to get the heavy bag off his sweaty head.

"Let's see if there's a light," said Sam.

But the room was windowless and completely dark. Its floor was covered with an inch of cold water that sloshed back and forth. Neil reached his arms in front of him, feeling for a light switch or doorway leading out. He tried listening for any noises outside the room.

"Where are we?" asked Biggs. Neil could hear him licking the last traces of candy from his arms.

"Somewhere where people can't find us, I bet," said Neil. He heard the faint sound of footsteps coming from above. His brain raced to think of a solution. "If we're still out at sea, maybe there's a way we can get in touch with Reboot."

"Not sure how," said Biggs. "Isn't his boat designed to be basically untraceable?"

"Yeah, good point," said Sam.

Neil swallowed hard. He needed to think of a way out.

"Oh, my phone!" said Sam.

Sam's phone!

"You have yours? Mine died on Reboot's boat," said Biggs.

"I turned it off to save the battery. With any luck there's still some juice in it," Sam said.

Neil could hear Sam fidgeting with her phone, and he watched the screen blink on. Her phone beeped with several incoming messages.

"Yes! This is gonna work!" Neil shouted.

"It's Corinne. She texted last night," Sam said.

"What'd she say?" asked Neil.

"Uh-oh," Sam said.

"What 'uh-oh'?" Neil said, worried. "What are we 'uh-oh'-ing?"

"This thing must've gotten damaged. Waterlogged or something," Sam said. She shook the phone furiously, but it didn't help. Tiny drops of water clung to the inside of the phone screen.

She did her best to read the message, but it was clouded with condensation. "She says she's sorry we had better things to do, so everybody left early."

Neil felt guilty—like, actually guilty. His friends had traveled all that way to meet at the convention—and then they were kicked out. All while he had the time of his life. The current situation seemed like fair payback.

Buzzzz.

With a defeated beep, Sam's phone died.

"Welp, that settles that. Guess there's no calling anybody," said Sam.

The cold water at their feet rushed forward as the boat's engine cut off. The floor stopped vibrating as the three paused in silence, unsure of what might happen next.

A metal hatch jerked open with a rusty squeak. Sunlight filtered into the room. Two muscled, bearded men in all-denim outfits looked down.

"Who said you could untie yourselves?" said one of them, who wore a gray stocking cap. He had a stubby nose that was slightly crooked.

"Never mind. Ze captain wants to see you," said the other. He had black hair with flecks of silver mixed in. They both spoke in thick French accents.

"What if we don't want to see the captain?" replied Neil.

"That eez not how this works," said the man in the hat.

Neil thought back to the small amount of karate wisdom his sister had passed on to him. *If they charge at us, what would Janey do? Go for the ankles?*

The two men turned and walked away, leaving the entrance open. An ocean breeze dipped into the stuffy room. The air was refreshing.

"What are you guys thinking?" said Biggs. "I'm worried there's, like, even bigger burlap bags waiting for us up there."

Neil's eyes narrowed.

Sam nodded at Neil. "Maybe it is a mission after all."

Neil knew they had no other option and climbed up the slimy metal ladder. He poked his head into the sunshine. There was no sign of the henchmen—or land, for that matter. Neil saw only stretches of unending ocean.

How far away from home are we?

Neil climbed out and turned to help Biggs and Sam. In stark contrast to the metal room they'd been in, the boat was a beautiful pearl-colored yacht. It was double the size of Reboot's and was filled with all sorts of sophisticated diving equipment.

Neil could see the ship wasn't like a regular boat with a large hull—it had a huge opening in the center, like a donut. A semitruck could fit through the center without scraping the sparkly paint job.

"This way, please," said one of the men, scowling. He pointed toward the cabin at the prow of the ship.

"Do we trust this?" asked Sam.

"More than jumping off and swimming home. The water could have sharks," said Neil. "Let's just see who this is."

Neil entered the surprisingly lavish cabin. Mirrors trimmed in gold were bolted to walls covered in amber wallpaper. The floor was covered in intricately stitched rugs with golden tassels. Expensive, very breakable-looking marble sculptures were perched in all corners of the room. It smelled like Neil's grandmother's house.

At the front of the cabin was an old-fashioned steering wheel and two albino parrots inside a large copper cage. A girl stood silhouetted by the window.

"Wow," Neil said. "Nice digs."

"Well, thank you," said the girl. She wore an intricate off-white dress. Its sleeves came down to her wrists in patterns that reminded Neil of his grandmother's couch doilies. It looked fancy.

"Who are you?" blurted Neil.

She stepped out from behind the large birdcage.

"Jolly?"

It was the host from Reboot's convention, without bright stage lights on her face.

The girl's eyes glistened as she gave a short laugh.

"I knew I'd get you here somehow," Jolly said. She walked to a cushy leather couch and sat, tapping the glass of a bottle containing a small model ship.

"What's going on?" asked Neil.

"I am the captain of this ship," she said. She spoke with a subtle accent—Neil wasn't sure where it was from, exactly, but it sounded British. She must've disguised it before. "Captain Jolly Rogers the Third."

"Do you kidnap all your guests, Captain Jolly?" asked Sam.

"Only in special circumstances like this," she said. "Sorry if my boys were a tad rough with you. They said you all seemed to be rather OK with being kidnapped, though."

Sam gave Neil a glare as the girl walked toward them with her hands on her hips. Around her slender neck was a thin gold chain with a locket.

"I need your help," said Jolly.

"What kind of help?" Neil asked. "Did Jones put you up to this?"

Neil was still hoping this could be some elaborate plan of the US government, setting them up for another covert operation.

"I don't know who this Jones is," Jolly said. "But you are correct about my game. I have a proposition for you three. Something I was going to ask you, before you rudely declined my invitation."

She led them back out to the middle of the ship. The three followed as a parrot squawked at Biggs. Biggs squawked back.

"I'm offering you the chance to pilot an experimental watercraft, the likes of which you've never seen." The young captain paused. "Well, on second thought, I guess you have seen it," Jolly said with a snort.

Bubbles began to emerge from the space between the two hulls of the ship. They intensified as a massive craft began to surface.

"Say hello to *Magda*," Jolly said when a huge metallic shark fin broke through the choppy water. "The megalodon."

"It does exist!" said Sam, shocked.

The monstrous mechanical shark was the size of three school buses. Salt water beaded on its gray exterior as its open jaws showed off rows of razor-sharp teeth. Each one was the size of a mailbox, and its jaws were big enough to tear a semitruck in half.

"And you three get the privilege of controlling it—in real life."

Neil was in shock. The fake hologram shark he'd controlled just the day before was very real—and he was going to drive it.

CHAPTER

8

A METAL MEGALODON! THIS COULD BE BETTER THAN JET fighters—or even spaceships.

Neil could tell this wasn't a government mission, but he was still ecstatic as he watched the shark move. Its rear fin wriggled back and forth, like a living shark's. When he looked closely, he could see the separate pieces of metal sheeting that had been bolted together, but it could easily be mistaken for the real deal.

"So you want us to drive that?" asked Sam.

Neil could see she was deep in thought about

something—she always scrunched her eyebrows together while concentrating.

"Correct, Samantha," said Jolly. She twirled a strand of her hair around her forefinger.

"It's actually just Sam."

"Excuse me, Sam," Jolly shot back. "Sorry again for having to snatch you up, but after showcasing my game all day, you three were the best of the best. No one came close to you."

Neil felt proud—they were, indeed, still the world's best gamers.

"I had to have you."

This feels . . . weird. Any video-game creator could surely pilot their own creation, right?

"Wait, if this is your ship, why can't you drive it?" Neil interrupted.

"Well, aren't we a bit eager," said Jolly, rolling her eyes. "This megalodon requires three people to command it. I can't leave my ship. So I'm trusting you to take over for me."

"So if we're driving this, ah, sharky-what-have-you-here, what's . . . the mission?" asked Biggs, gesturing toward the beast. "You never told us what we're actually going to be doing."

The girl paused and frowned. "Oh, it's simple—to help with the aquarium I'm building in honor of my family."

"What happened to your family?" asked Sam.

The captain cleared her throat. "They were . . . they're no longer here, is all you need to know," said Jolly.

"Well, we're here to help. So are we, like, picking up forty-gallon tanks for you?" Biggs asked. "Because if so, I tried raising turtles a couple years back and they sort of, ah, escaped. So if you're looking for a turtle tank, have I got a deal for you!"

"Are you sure you don't have a few screws loose?" Jolly asked Biggs.

"Oh, they've been lost for a while now," Biggs defended himself.

"If you must know, we're collecting sharks."

"Can you do that?" asked Sam.

"We can do whatever we want," Jolly said, smiling devilishly. "We're going to take every shark we see."

"What? Why would you do that?!" yelled Biggs. "That would ruin all sea life as we know it. Don't you know how an ecosystem works?"

"Of course I do," the captain said. "That's why I need

them in my aquarium. I need to collect *every* shark we can find."

"Then if you know what an ecosystem is, you should be smart enough to know this is an awful idea," Biggs said. There was a frustration in his voice that Neil had never heard before. This wasn't a joke anymore, and this was definitely not something that Jones had organized. "Sharks are very important. They're just misunderstood."

"Misunderstood?" Jolly barked. "I think I definitely understand the fact that sharks are responsible for me being alone."

Jolly's hands curled into tiny fists. She spoke quickly, without the restrained calm she'd displayed the day before.

"Some people will never understand," the captain said. "Do you know what it's like to be alone?"

"Totally. The other day I didn't go online until after dinner," said Biggs.

"I'm beginning to wonder if I took the wrong people," said Jolly. "I thought you were geniuses."

"Oh, we are," said Neil, defending his friend. "And if *you're* so smart, how are you gonna house every shark? I hate to break it to you, but there's, like, a lot of sharks out there. You can't bait them by chumming every ocean."

Jolly gave another piercing laugh. "Chum, that horrid bloody mess, is like shark broccoli."

"Huh?" said Neil, frustrated.

"They like it but don't love it," Jolly said. "Shark parents just force their kids to eat it."

"What makes you a shark expert, then, huh?" asked Neil.

"Because my parents were the most knowledgeable shark experts in the world. And sharks are the reason they are gone," Jolly said, stamping her foot. "I've studied everything I could about the dreadful beasts."

Neil grew quiet. He had been growing frustrated with Jolly, but her story sounded tragic. He imagined what he would do if his own family had been eaten by sharks. It wasn't fair, but did Jolly really need revenge? There had to be another way.

"I'm sorry to hear that," said Sam. "Really."

"Me too," Jolly said, exhaling loudly. "Apologies for my outburst." She took a deep breath and looked up. "Some beautiful cumulonimbus clouds out today. Means something's brewing."

"So how do you plan on finding sharks?" he asked.

"Ketchup," Jolly said.

Neil and Sam laughed.

"Like, French-fry ketchup?" said Neil, dipping an invisible fry in an invisible cup of the red tomato mixture.

"From some lowly squeeze bottle? Don't be crude," said Jolly.

"What other kind of ketchup is there?" Biggs said.

"The caviar of ketchup."

"Is that just, like, a bigger cup of it?" Biggs asked.

The girl glared back at him.

"And sharks really like that stuff?"

"Trust me. I've spent years studying a shark's sense of smell," Jolly said. "I know that there are ancient ketchups from Japan and Indonesia that sharks can smell across entire seas."

Neil thought that might actually be true. He didn't really know how the whole ocean jet stream thing worked, but knew they had currents spanning hundreds of miles. Plus he loved ketchup—why wouldn't sharks?

"So, good for you with your ketchup and all, but what are you gonna do if we won't play along with your awful mission?" asked Sam. "Because there's no way we're going after sharks."

"Then I hope you enjoyed your time in the brig,"

Jolly said. She whistled, and her henchmen appeared. "Pierre, Fabien—our friends need another time-out."

With a snap, Jolly's henchmen swooped down on the three gamers. One grabbed Neil and Sam, while the other secured a flailing Biggs. They were dragged back to the cold metal room. Jolly followed, standing over Neil.

"You'll come around," she said. "Pierre, shut them in."

"Au revoir," said Jolly's goon with the hairier knuckles. He slammed the latch shut, leaving the group in total darkness once again. Neil huddled together with his friends, unsure of where he'd gone wrong.

CHAPTER

9

★ ★ ★

AFTER THE FIFTH ATTEMPT AT KICKING OPEN THE HATCH, Neil, Sam, and Biggs collapsed back onto the metal bench, sweaty, tired, and angry.

"Something tells me we're gonna be stuck in here forever," said Sam.

Forever is maybe a bit much. I'm sure she'd feed us to sharks before then.

"Yeah, this is less than cool," added Biggs. "If video games make me have to hurt sharks, then maybe I'm done with video games."

That was like hearing a superstar athlete discuss early retirement.

"Guys, I agree," Neil said. "I'm sorry this happened, really—but I bet she would've kidnapped us regardless. She was begging to take us after we played her game. At least maybe this means that the others got home safe."

Sam groaned. "You're right. But why does being the best always get us into trouble?"

A big wave rolled past Jolly's ship, and the three friends felt their stomachs leap up a foot. Neil was growing tired of life at sea.

"So what should we do, then?" Sam asked. "Help her destroy every shark alive?"

"Any new inventions that might help us out, Biggs?" Neil asked his friend. Maybe he had another bright idea, like the ones from his smellable gaming and universal sign language.

"Sorry, Neil," Biggs said, defeated. "It's been a slow year for inventions."

Neil bit at the inside of his cheek, hoping his brain would suddenly think of a perfect plan. He wished he had the rest of the team with him. It would be helpful to use the sharp thinking of JP and the Olde Worlde knowledge of Riley. Neil thought of the last time he had seen them, during their winning streak of Shark Hunt.

The game. Something with the game?

"Maybe there's a cheat code from the game we can use," offered Neil. "Something that will make the megalodon explode so she can't succeed."

"A: Do you remember using a cheat code?" said a defensive Sam. "B: If that shark explodes with us in it, what happens?"

"And H: Robot-shark explosions have been known to erode all types of coral," followed Biggs. "We can't risk something like that."

Neil let out a long breath.

"I mean, what else is there?" Neil said. "We'll be stuck down here for a long time before she'll feel any type of sympathy for us."

"I got a weird vibe from her, too," said Biggs.

Neil dropped his voice to just above a whisper. "If she really designed that video game, why is she having other people do the work?"

"So you think she doesn't know how to steer her own machine?" Biggs asked. "It seemed to be working earlier."

"That could just be autopilot," Neil said. "You guys remember that game—it took all three of us to control it. It was pretty tricky. Is she, like, only in charge of ketchup?"

"Guys, we have to do it," said Biggs. "In order to save every shark. I'd rather have us be involved than trust any of the other players she auditioned. I think we can stop her and save the day. We've done it before!"

"You sure?" asked Sam. "Something goes wrong and we chomp down on a bunch of sharks. Plus we don't have backup from Jones."

"We'll be careful. I know we will," said Biggs. "And maybe when we're on the radio, we can try and contact Jones or the White House."

"If you say so, Biggs," Neil replied softly. He felt another wave sweep under them.

"There's a huge aquarium in Monterey, north up the coast," said Biggs. "We can drop off the sharks we catch in a safe location and get the aquarium's help."

Neil tried to think of a better option, but he was fresh out of ideas.

"Sounds like a plan."

★ ★ ★

"Jolly!" the three screamed through the crack of the hatch. A few seconds passed before they heard the sound of footsteps overhead. The door was ripped open by Pierre.

"We'll do it," Neil said.

Jolly stepped between the two burly men and put her boot heel on the edge of the hatch. "I have your word?" the girl asked.

"All our words. Whichever ones you like best," Neil replied. "Now get us out of here. It smells like rotten seaweed in this thing."

The three captives crawled up the metal ladder to the deck. It was getting windy.

"I knew you'd eventually see things my way," Jolly replied, putting a hand on Neil's and Sam's shoulders.

As the boat wobbled, Jolly walked them into her cabin. Neil sat down on a leather couch that was so comfortable, he nearly forgot he'd just agreed to destroy all sharks.

"Do you think we could try this famous ketchup of yours? Before we start? I wanted to see what's so cool about it," Neil said.

Jolly's eyebrows perked up. "Of course." She snapped

her fingers and Pierre returned with a small wooden crate. He cracked the top off.

"Careful now," said Jolly as a jar was hoisted from a nest of Bubble Wrap. "This is an expensive delicacy."

She held a red container with a metal lid. It was smaller than a two-liter bottle of soda. Something was written in Japanese on the side, just under a picture of a small sea creature. Neil had no clue what it was, but it looked like a tiny shrimp.

"What kind of ketchup is this again?" asked Neil.

"A secret Japanese ketchup recipe, but perfected by my family over generations," Jolly said. "My great-grandmother discovered it during her pirate days. Her son, my grandfather, created and ran our first factory."

"For ketchup?"

"Absolutely. Using recipes plundered by the first Jolly Rogers."

Neil waved his hand over the bottle, inhaling the peculiar smell. It reminded him of the seaweed candy his friend Tyler would eat during after-school robot building.

"So what's in it?" Sam asked.

"How precious. I could never give that away," Jolly said. "But I will let you in on our key ingredient: krill."

--

"Krill ketchup?" said Sam.

"A bit unconventional, yes. But you can't beat the results; it's a famous delicacy in certain circles. A jar like this can go for ten thousand euros. And the Russians love it."

Jolly unscrewed the top of the ketchup jar. Its lid clicked open with a satisfying *pop*, and the aroma of bizarre ketchup filled the air.

"Care for a taste?" the captain offered, plunging a finger into the dark-red sauce. She licked it and handed the jar to Biggs. "It's right tasty."

Neil dipped a finger in and sucked it clean.

Oh, not that bad really. More spicy than anything.

"You wouldn't happen to know if these krill were free-range, would you?" Biggs asked, studying the Japanese print running along the side of the ketchup container.

"Just taste the ketchup, string bean," said Jolly. "But not too much. Dipping a finger in is about fifty dollars' worth."

Biggs ran his pinkie across the top of the gloppy red mixture.

"Very nice—I'm getting some hints of heirloom

tomato," Biggs said, licking his lips like a reality-TV food critic. "Maybe some Doritos, as well?"

Jolly gave Biggs a stare capable of melting glaciers.

"Sam?" offered Biggs.

"Well, I'm a veggie-saurus, so I'll pass. But Jolly, as a fellow dinosaur lover, I did have a few questions about your huge shark," Sam said, cranking up the charm. "It's literally the coolest thing I've ever seen. Did you model it off a living great white? What are the teeth made of?"

Jolly's face lit up.

"Are you a fan of Cenozoic-era vertebrates, too?" the captain asked.

"You better believe it, sister," Sam replied. "At home, I have four fossils of actual dinosaurs that date back millions and million years."

"Then I've got to show you the jaws," Jolly said, putting an arm tenderly around Sam's shoulders. "I had our top-secret krill-collecting submersible modified. I copied the serrated edges of actual shark teeth and just made them four times as big."

"Whoa," said Sam.

The two walked out onto the deck, with Biggs and Neil trailing behind.

- -

"Now let's do this, shall we?" said Jolly, turning to Biggs and Neil. She seemed to be much friendlier when things were going her way.

She walked the crew outside and down to the end of the ship, next to the head of the mechanical shark-eating shark. With heavy steps, Pierre and Fabien followed.

"You collect nothing but sharks, understood?" Jolly said. "Inside this vessel is a tank that can hold up to three hundred sharks, all to be deposited at the new facility near San Diego."

"Hey, that's where we were," said Sam. "I thought you said it was an aquarium?"

"Right," said Jolly. She stiffened, and her thin nostrils flared. "Aquarium."

"That didn't look like an aquarium is all."

"Once it's finished, you'll see," said Jolly. She pivoted back to her shark creation, *Magda*. It was barely three feet away, and Neil reached out his hand to touch it. It felt slimy enough to be real. Its eyes glowed a deep red. The dorsal fin was the size of a sail from a small boat. Neil had never witnessed anything so powerful, and he'd been to Mars, so that was saying something.

Jolly clicked a tiny remote in her hand, and a hatch just behind the gills opened.

"Climb aboard, crew," said Jolly. "You'll see you're well acquainted with the controls. Glad to have you on my team."

Neil felt uneasy. It might have been the churning sea, or the overwhelming amount of last night's candy in his gut, but Neil knew it was a feeling that this wasn't going to end well.

CHAPTER
10

"SO WHERE'D YOU'D DESIGN THESE CONTROLS?" ASKED NEIL, sitting in the middle of the three captain's chairs. "Did you base it off other simulators?"

He was full of questions, nervous energy, exotic candy, and a tiny bit of rare ketchup. He shifted in the uncomfortable seat. It felt like sitting on a metal beam and looked like a dentist's chair plucked from a nightmare. Metal bars, like a roller-coaster safety harness, were above each seat. Fabien and Pierre had followed them inside but had to hunch over in the cramped quarters. Jolly stood behind them while Neil and his friends were harnessed in, making sure never to lift a finger to help.

"Did I base what off other simulations?" said a distracted Jolly.

"Your game, the controls," Neil said. "This really looks like Shark Hunt; it's impressive that you captured it so well."

"Sure," she said.

For a designer, she's not very eager to talk games.

Neil was cramped. He felt like he was in a cage. Even the headsets they wore were too small, and the metal wires of the mouthpiece kept rubbing at Neil's chin. The floors were metal grates, and Neil could hear the inner workings of the prehistoric mecha shark below.

"And safety bars down," said Jolly.

Fabien and Pierre pulled them down, covering their chests and shoulders and making sure all three made an intimidating click.

"Extra tight—don't want anybody thinking they can get up," said the captain.

Neil pushed up on the bar, which didn't budge. He was trapped in Jolly's real-life shark hunt.

"Et voilà," said Fabien.

"We can't get up? What if something goes wrong? Or this thing fills with water?" Sam said.

"There are emergency procedures, but they won't be needed."

"What about bathroom breaks?" added Biggs.

"We'll handle bathroom breaks on a case-by-case basis," said Jolly, leaning her head toward the only exit. "No more questions."

She clicked the remote in her hand, and the gills of the ship closed tight.

"That's possibly the worst restroom strategy I've ever heard," said Biggs, examining the set of controls in front of him.

He was on Neil's right, with Sam on the other side. A homemade console of gauges was laid out in front of them. The nose of the megalodon must've been high-tech one-way glass, because Neil was looking straight into the ocean.

The ceiling was metal grating as well, with a few electrical cords and wires slipping through its cracks. It reminded Neil a bit of a NASA-designed craft. Nothing was pretty, but it all combined to make something special.

"Can you guys hear me?" asked Jolly through the headsets.

"Loud and clear," said Neil.

"I'll be with you over the radio, and don't worry, it's a closed line. Don't get any ideas of calling your precious parents or anything."

Neil thought back to his family back home, probably hanging out watching Janey practice her karate moves. Part of him wished he'd just stayed home, instead of getting into this mess.

"I will be watching every move on the video feed. So no funny business," continued Jolly. "Everything functioning properly?"

They tested the ship's controls. They were nearly identical to the game they'd played the day before. Sam controlled diving and rising to the surface, while Neil controlled steering via the pectoral fins. Biggs commanded the speed of *Magda*, too, by gauging the force from the tail fin.

Biggs accelerated and the shark lurched forward. They were now in open water, swimming ahead of Jolly's yacht.

They found their bearings with the craft, gently guiding the shark down and then back up to the surface of the water. Neil watched a pack of curious dolphins swim alongside them.

"Cool," said Neil. "They're probably wondering where this thing has been for millions of years."

Biggs pushed them faster, leaving two rippling waves in *Magda*'s wake.

Without seeing the rest of the huge mechanical megalodon behind him, Neil could've believed this was an actual video game.

"Let's try a barrel roll!" said Sam as she jerked her controls hard to the left.

The shark twisted in the water with grace.

"All right, good to see you're already enjoying it," said Jolly over the radio frequency. "It looks like radar is showing a school of sharks a bit west of here. Let's start heading there."

While Neil still didn't like the idea of going after sharks, getting to let loose on the controls was exhilarating. Biggs pushed forward on the metal acceleration lever. *Magda* instantly thrashed its tail fin, swimming like an actual shark.

"It's like flying a jet, only the water is the sky," said Biggs. "I just blew my own mind."

"How, exactly, would you know what flying a jet is like?" asked Jolly from the radio. Biggs looked at the glass bubble camera monitoring them from the ceiling.

"Ugh, video games of course. You know what I mean," said Biggs.

"You kids sure do love your fancy video games," Jolly said.

"And you don't?" said Sam.

"There are so many more interesting things in the world," Jolly said. "It's a pity you people waste your lives staring at screens."

"OK, Jolly, what's your deal?" said Neil. "For someone who has a video game named after them, you seem to hate them. I didn't see a screen larger than three inches on your ship. Something's not adding up."

"You think that game was for anything other than finding recruits?" Jolly said, starting to sound angry.

Wait, it's not a real game?

"And I'll tell you what's not adding up: the fact that we haven't captured a single shark. My radar is showing a small pack of hammerheads a few hundred meters from here. Now turn left."

Magda kept its course, heading straight. Neil, Sam,

and Biggs didn't budge from their present course.

"I said left!" shouted Jolly. A small electric shock coursed through the metal of the three pilot seats.

"Ow!" yelped Sam. "What's going on?"

"Let's call it positive reinforcement," said Jolly with a snort.

The ship veered left as Sam maneuvered a fin. Neil's hands began to sweat as his nerves still buzzed from the jolt. Jolly was more sinister than she seemed.

"Good," said Jolly. "Now I trust you'll do as I say from now on. Head for the grouping of sharks."

"You know, if you're making an aquarium, I can suggest much cooler stuff to collect," said an upset Biggs. "There's far more interesting sea life."

"You really are something special, aren't you," Jolly said. "You worry about doing what you're told. Give me full speed!"

She sent another electric jolt and gave the jaws a few quick chomps. Unlike in the video game, Jolly made sure she was the only person in charge of the jaws.

"No, I won't," Biggs said, his voice shaky. "You mean there's no aquarium?"

"You think revenge for my family is a little glass

viewing booth for those monsters?" Jolly said. "We're getting them out of every ocean. Forever. Now shape up, or would you like to see how many volts you can take?"

Neil gulped. He knew they were in deep trouble, literally.

CHAPTER

11

"SO WHAT'S OUR PLAN?" SAM PUT A HAND IN FRONT OF HER microphone so Jolly couldn't hear her.

Neil shrugged his shoulders, covering his headset as well.

"I don't think we'll make it north to that aquarium," Neil whispered. Biggs nodded in agreement.

"Only if we want to be extra crispy, well done," said Biggs. "But we can't let her have control of this thing."

"We need to find a way to make this megalodon extinct," said Sam. "Again."

"Copy that," said Neil. "Let's see what we can do. Sorry in advance for getting you both electrocuted."

"It's worth it," said Biggs. Sam gave a nod.

The trio guided the shark toward coordinates given by Jolly, which seemed to keep her silent. Neil knew he wasn't ready to withstand another burst of electricity. The amount of sugar inside of him would most likely act as some kind of superconductor.

The team accelerated forward, and soon a group of sharks slowly became visible in the watery distance. They all circled in a feeding frenzy. Smaller sharks darted between the larger, slow-moving ones. From her controls, Jolly opened the jaws of *Magda*.

"Full speed ahead!" commanded the captain.

But before Jolly clamped the jaws shut, Neil guided the nose of the ship away from the cluster of swimming sharks. He felt a shock course through his body but kept the open jaws of *Magda* away from the sharks.

"What happened!" Jolly yelled, gnashing the teeth of the mechanical animal. They coasted past craggy rock formations and coral, leaving behind a trail of bubbles.

"I lost control! Maybe we're just not as good as you thought," fibbed Neil.

- -

"Don't lie to me, Neil," Jolly said, her voice eerily calm. "I know what you're capable of."

"Lie to you? But—"

"Oh, arguing is pointless," Jolly interrupted. "Let's just bring the sharks to us, shall we? Then I can escort you all to the brig—permanently."

"Fabien, I think it's time to deploy the ketchup," Jolly said to her henchman. "The finest Rogers Ketchup has to offer."

There was a moment's silence.

Rogers Ketchup. That's actually a name from my nightmares.

Neil remembered, clearly, that the brand was the sponsor of the Southwestern Robotics Invitational. He suddenly realized why Jolly's laugh had been so familiar—she must have been the one watching from the wings. He didn't know what to say. Was Jolly just really into homemade electronics? Had she been following him for months?

"Jolly, just so you know, your ketchup is horrible," Biggs said. "And your krill stuff tastes like feet."

"Well, aren't we feeling talkative," said Jolly. "Lucky for us, sharks have a taste for feet."

"For the last time, we're not killing sharks!" Biggs

screamed. He was, for the first time ever, angry—like, *angry.*

Neil knew he had to do something. His mind raced, trying to think of something from Jolly's video game to use against her.

"If you won't do what I command, someone else will," Jolly explained. "Do you *know* how many kids lined up to play that game? And right now we've got shipments of ketchup going out to strategically lure sharks to me. I can force someone else to collect them for me, once I get rid of you."

Neil saw an outcropping of rocks ahead. A few formed a huge arch, which crawled with dozens of sharks all looking for their next meal. He winced as the jaws of *Magda* opened wide, ready to scoop them up.

"Hey, guys, you think Jolly was serious about some kind of escape pod being on this thing?" Neil said, putting a hand in front of his headset microphone.

"Um, maybe?"

"Well, let's hope. We need to make a move right now."

For the first time in twelve hours, Neil felt something good inside his stomach—a kind of fire like when he first climbed into a Chameleon's cockpit.

"Let's break this thing," said Neil. "If we go down, we're going down fighting."

He wiggled in the chair and readjusted his grip on the rubber joystick. Sam and Biggs did the same, but a jolt of electricity ran through them again.

"Ow! OK, OK, we're going," said Biggs.

"Jolly, let's do this," Neil said confidently into the microphone.

"Head for those rocks!" shouted the evil captain.

"Roger that."

Neil guided *Magda* toward a flurry of sharks, but he reached a foot over to control Sam's fin. The megalodon swerved toward the naturally formed arch. It would barely be big enough for the fake shark to squeeze through.

Jolly sent another shock through the metal chairs, and it vibrated Neil all the way down to his teeth.

"Stay strong, everybody!" shouted Neil, mostly for his own sake. He kept a firm grip on the control stick and steered the shark into the arch. Jolly screamed into the radio headsets.

With a huge screech, Neil felt the dorsal fin of the submarine shark connect with the rocks above. Neil and friends let out a huge cheer as the ship began to lose its balance.

"Neil, you're breaking it. You're doing it!" exclaimed Sam.

"Critical injury," said a robotic computer voice. Gauges and meters began to misfire from every control panel.

Without a properly functioning dorsal fin, *Magda* was spinning endlessly. It spiraled like a football. Neil was getting dizzy, unable to focus on a fixed spot to reduce his nausea.

There's way too much ketchup inside me for this to end well.

Suddenly the metal bars holding the pilots in disengaged. With a hydraulic hiss, Neil, Biggs, and Sam were released.

"Hold on tight, everybody!" yelled Sam. She regained control of her fin and managed to slow the rolling of the ship, wedging her radio headset next to the joystick. Blue emergency lights illuminated the back of the cockpit. They surrounded a small doorway marked with a giant red exclamation point.

"Oh, you're all soon to be smithereens. You think you can get away in *my* ship?" came Jolly's voice. She continued to scream as the three friends staggered away from their seats.

"That's gotta be the escape pod," said Neil. "Let's make a break for it, before this thing sinks."

The three friends grabbed metal beams to help stabilize themselves. The shark kept twisting through the water like a torpedo. Neil peered out the windows to see an orange coral reef ahead.

"Turn with it!" said Sam, who maneuvered around the spinning cockpit, walking on the wall and then ceiling as if they were back in space. They scrambled to the back of the ship's cabin and crawled into the tiny escape shuttle. There was barely enough room for all three to fit, but Sam pulled the metal latch shut. A red handle was illuminated behind a clear piece of plastic. Sam removed the cover and tugged on the emergency release.

"Let's get out of here!" yelled Sam as she maxed out every lever on the tiny craft. With an incredible burst of speed, the small submarine sped away from *Magda*.

The shark continued to roll, grinding its fin on yet another rock formation—narrowly missing a head-on collision with the coral.

Neil's face was squeezed against a small window. He watched as the shark's eyes flickered off and then back on again. With a final crackle, they turned black, and the nose of the submersible began to sink.

"Guys, I think we just pulled off an impossible escape," Sam said. "I'm shaking."

"Me too," said Neil.

"Me three," said Biggs. "But there's a good chance that's red Singapore-goo related."

"Now let's get away from her before her yacht catches up," said Sam.

Neil smiled as the tiny submarine sputtered its way through the ocean, past lots of happily uneaten sharks.

CHAPTER 12

"SO, WE'RE IN A SUBMARINE," SAID BIGGS, HIS LEGS BENT to fit. "A submarine that is stuck somewhere in the ocean, surrounded by sharks, and we don't have to be at school until tomorrow. What's next?"

Biggs was right. It was probably noon, and regular life continued tomorrow morning. The team paused as the sub's propellers continued to hum. The pod was controlled by a simple joystick and two buttons—one to stop, the other to go. It was like a prehistoric video game.

They coasted through open water, with schools of

small translucent fish wriggling alongside. Various sizes and species of sharks swam past, coming close enough to investigate.

"And what do we do about Jolly?" asked Sam.

Neil wasn't sure, but he knew getting away was the priority.

"Let's take things one step at a time. For instance, how far can this thing get us? Can't imagine there's much fuel in an escape pod," Neil said. He scanned the controls for some kind of fuel monitor, but there was nothing to be seen.

Sam read from a GPS. "Well, we're somewhere in the Pacific, pretty far out, though. We definitely don't have enough fuel to make it back to California."

"Unless we—" Neil said, thinking aloud. "Nah, it'd be too much of a long shot."

"No, say it," Biggs answered. "Whatcha thinking? Does it involve a family of friendly sea lions? 'Cause if so, we're on the same wavelength."

"Ha," Neil laughed. "Biggs, don't take this the wrong way, but I'm not sure anybody will ever be on your same wavelength."

"Good—I don't want it to get crowded."

"But I was thinking," Neil continued. "We've got to be close to that island with Harris's warehouse, right?"

"Neil Andertol, you're a genius!" Sam said.

"Now I'm not totally sure, but I think we could find it," Neil continued. "If we only knew the coordinates."

"Done," Sam said proudly.

"What?" Neil asked. Sam rested her hand over a tiny numeric keypad on the ship's control panel.

"Latitude and longitude are plugged in. After our Chameleon mission, I went online to try and find the island from a satellite," she said. "You could barely see it, but I memorized the coordinates, just in case we ever had the chance to go back."

"Well done, soldier," said Neil as he watched a flashing dot appeared on the radar.

"That's where we need to be," said Sam. "Now let's just hope this little thing can get us there."

"Oh, there's a radio," Neil said. "Maybe this one works."

He found the simple switch for the radio. The small speaker sizzled to life. "We need to let somebody know what a maniac Jolly Rogers is."

Neil held on to the plastic receiver of the radio,

which was tethered to the control panel by a spiral black rubber cord. "Hello? Anybody there?"

There was no response, so Neil unplugged it.

"Just in case she's tracking us or something," Neil said. "We'll get in touch with the others once we get to Harris's place."

He looked at the console holding the radio and saw the logo for Harris's family company, Beed Industries.

"Interesting," Neil mumbled. Soon, the small chain of islands began to appear on the sub's radar.

"There they are!" said Neil. "Sam Gonzales, you are a genius."

"I just hope we can get there," she said.

As the escape pod charged toward the chain of small islands, it began to sputter. There'd been barely any fuel in the tank when they'd started, and now it was bone-dry. The sub slowly coasted forward only off momentum.

The lights of the cockpit dimmed as the sub started to sink.

"Uh-oh, c'mon, baby," said Biggs, tapping the dashboard of the small submarine. Amazingly, the craft mustered one final push forward. Their heads jerked forward as they collided nosefirst with the sandy shore of the smallest island in the chain. Neil opened the hatch leading out and fought small waves as the cockpit filled with water. The three splashed out of the submarine and crawled to the shore. They lay out on their backs, all of them still pulsing with adrenaline.

"I've never felt so happy to be on a beach," said Sam. Neil, and his stomach, agreed. He closed his eyes for a moment, letting the warm sun beat down on his face. He heard a familiar ostrich noise and opened his eyes.

"Hey, this is Weo's place!" Neil said, excitedly looking around. It was a place Neil had crash-landed on before. "He can help us get in touch with somebody."

If anyone will help us, it's Weo. Unless he's riding an ostrich somewhere. Then this could get interesting.

"We could even make a phone call from Penny's Pizza," Neil said, his nerves settling at the thought of delicious pineapple. "I think I know how to get us there."

After twenty minutes of cutting through thorny trees, the group reached the vine net Neil had once called home for a few hours.

"No way, it's still here!" Neil said. The netting was overgrown with moss and looked like it was now a nest for a small family of birds. Weo's tree house was in a similar condition. Vines were beginning to wind their way between the wooden slats of the floor.

"Weo!" Neil yelled as Sam and Biggs finally caught up. "Weo?" There was no answer, apart from the song of the island's tropical birds.

Neil was getting a bit worried.

He walked toward the wooden ladder that led to the tree house. As he climbed each rung, it groaned under his body weight. Neil reached the top and walked the handmade gangplank, his shoes kicking dust through the cracks of wooden slats. It looked like nobody had been there in years—even though Neil had visited six months ago.

"Maybe he's somewhere else," Neil shouted down to Sam and Biggs. "It's empty."

"Or maybe this whole place is deserted?" said Sam. "I don't see too many signs of life. Unless you count the monkeys that keep trying to steal my hair bands."

"Let's continue looking around," Neil answered. "Where else could he be? You don't think anything . . . bad happened?"

The three climbed down from the tree house and walked to the top of the island's rocky hill. They looked toward Harris's island. A chorus of birds squawked from across the small channel of water.

The ostriches had migrated from Weo's island to the Feather Duster warehouse and had taken over. Ostriches poked around the island's open spaces, leaving things filthy, covered with eggshells and bird droppings.

"Let's start hoofing it," Neil said. Neil could feel the sun beginning to crisp his fair skin. Still wearing the white uniform from Reboot Robiskie's party yacht, Neil Andertol began to walk over the sandbars leading to the home of the Feather Duster warehouse.

Neil knew finding his friend could at least help solve the problem of getting home. Where there was Weo, you were bound to find Harris. Where there was Harris, there was a private jet.

We can also see what he knows about Jolly, and why Beed Industries helped build that submarine.

CHAPTER

13

THE FEATHER DUSTER WAREHOUSE SMELLED LIKE NEIL'S garage, dusty and full of smelly fertilizer. Neil could see a single light filtering out through a window on the second floor.

"Do you think that's the main office? Who could be up there?" Neil asked, getting the creeps.

"Maybe it's Mr. Beed?" Sam suggested.

They headed toward a freight elevator bay and pushed the up arrow. The doors opened and closed with a pleasant chime.

The lift offered two buttons: *W*, the floor they were on, and *P*.

"Ooh, where to go?" said Biggs, stepping alongside Neil in the elevator.

"Gotta be the presidential suite," said Biggs, who pushed the *P* button with an excited finger. They started to move up. "If Mr. Beed is there, this could be a good time to get some feedback on the smell technology he bought from me. I've been trying to set up a meeting for months."

Neil glanced at his watch. It was seven P.M. back home in Colorado. After some quick mental math, he realized he had roughly twelve hours to save every living shark before getting to homeroom. He probably needed to give his parents an update, too.

Ding.

The silver doors of the elevator rushed open to reveal a plush office. It was shaped like a lima bean and had blue shag carpeting. Every surface was covered in ostrich knickknacks. Pictures. Figurines. Slippers. In the center of the room was an L-shaped yellow couch that had ostrich legs for armrests. A single ostrich-shaped lamp gave the room an eerie glow.

Neil, Sam, and Biggs walked toward the mahogany desk. A leather chair with a tall back was turned away from them.

"Uh, hello, President Beed?" said Biggs. "My name is Robert Starlight Hurbigg, and I'm here to talk smells and sharks."

There was no response. They walked around the desk to see the chair was empty.

"President Beed?" Biggs continued. From behind a closed door came the sound of water splashing in a sink.

"Somebody's in the bathroom," Neil whispered.

Before they could hide, the bathroom door opened.

"Weo?" blurted Neil.

The boy who walked out looked startled.

"No way! Neil!" said Weo. He wore fresh jeans and a yellow button-down shirt with the Feather Duster logo stitched on its front. His hair was nicely trimmed, and he flashed an electric smile. He looked good, as if he'd been sleeping indoors or something.

"What happened to the tree house?"

"Well, I'm in here now," Weo said. "The islands had an earthquake not too long ago, and the house was feeling sketchy. And all the killer surf got destroyed. It's nothing but rocky shore now, so everybody bailed."

Weo sat down in the padded chair behind the comically large desk.

"So what happened with Harris?"

"Things are good with me and Harris, but a lot of employees left once the pizza place closed."

Neil let out an involuntary gasp. "No!"

"Penny's Pizza closed?" Biggs said, defeated.

"Yeah, I know it's a tragedy. Penny found another island where she could set up shop," Weo said. "And Harris wanted to spend less time here and needed somebody to manage the facility. I'm in charge of the whole warehouse right now."

He twirled his hand in a circle. Neil looked at the boy's desk. It had only a framed picture of Weo and Harris and a bronze rectangular nameplate that read PRESIDENT AND WEO.

"You're in charge now? At least that's awesome news!" Neil congratulated him. "The place looks much nicer than before."

"Thanks," said Weo. He cocked his head to the side. "So what are you guys doing here? Again?"

"It's a long story," said Neil. "But we need to get

- -

home as soon as possible. And talk to our friends, and alert international shark authorities—and the president."

Weo gave him a puzzled look.

"A crazy girl named Jolly is out in the ocean somewhere right now, trying to capture every shark in existence."

"What? Like, every shark?" gasped Weo. "That would destroy sea life as we know it."

"And she's got some kind of secret ketchup to trap them. We've got to stop her before she goes through with her plan," Neil explained.

"Weo, can we use your phone?" asked Sam. "I should also tell my parents I won't make dinner. And figure out what my excuse is for why I'm late. . . ."

"You guys are more than free to use anything," Weo said. He pointed to the black phone on his desk.

"Thanks—you're a lifesaver," said Sam. She picked up the phone while Neil and Biggs continued talking with Weo.

"Weo, I'm not sure if I'm doing this right, but I don't think the phone's working," said Sam.

"That's odd," Weo said. He walked next to Sam and investigated. "Yeah, no dial tone or anything."

Weo turned to his computer and attempted to go online or view email.

"Weird," Weo said. "Looks like everything is down."

"It's Jolly," said Neil. "I bet she's blocking all signals so that we can't contact anyone. Our radio on the sub didn't work either!"

"I'd offer to take you all home, really, but I can't leave," Weo said. "In case anything goes wrong around here, I have to stick around—but . . ."

The boy cocked his head, as if he was listening for a distant noise.

"But I might know someone who can take you guys. Come with me."

Weo walked to the rooftop terrace adjacent to his office. Neil, Biggs, and Sam followed Weo outside. It was covered in vibrant plant life and looked out over the small chain of islands. The sound of a jet engine filled the afternoon air.

A Beed Industries private jet landed on the roof's small landing strip. Its engines were slowly winding down as the rear passenger door popped open. A skinny frame filled the doorway as Harris poked his head outside.

"Weo, my good man," said Harris. His arms were

full of RebootCon gift bags. "Come give me a hand with these, will you? I think I snagged every game coming out for the next two years."

Harris dropped his armload of bags when he finally saw the crowd that was with Weo.

"Whoa, fancy seeing you guys here," Harris said, wiping a few smudges from his sunglasses. "You guys have a good night? Sink Reboot's yacht?"

"Quit the friendly act, Harris," said Neil. Harris looked startled.

"Lovely seeing you as well, Neil."

Neil was angry that his friend could betray him.

"Tell us everything you know about Jolly Rogers," Neil demanded. "Or else."

CHAPTER

14

HARRIS BEED LOOKED UNEASY.

"Now settle down, Neil," said Harris, clearly thrown by the accusations. "No need to go around 'or else'-ing people."

"I don't want to hear it. I need to know what you know about Jolly Rogers, starting with, for example, why Beed Industries helped build her monster shark."

Neil was right in Harris's face. His jaw was clenched—they had met Harris as an evil villain, after all. It would be easy for him to still be up to no good.

"Calm down, Neil," Harris said. He put his sunglasses on top of his head. He looked at Weo, who was sitting in his desk chair. "Somebody needs less sugar."

"While that may be true, I still need answers," Neil replied.

Harris put his hands out to try and calm down his friend. "I'll tell you what I know about her. But let me first say, her family's and my family's companies have done business for decades. We're contracted to make lots of things for them."

"Like what?"

"Ketchup-manufacturing equipment."

"Really? Including the robotic shark?"

"Exactly!" said Harris. "'Krill collectors,' as my dad calls them. We worked with the Rogers family to create the top-of-the-line technology."

"This sounds like an easy excuse for another evil plan," Neil said. "Am I the only one who thinks it's fishy Beed Industries could be involved somehow?"

"Neil, remember what Jolly was saying when she showed us *Magda*?" Sam said. "She modified one of the sharks they use to catch krill."

"Jolly's parents created it in a certain way so that

it wouldn't disrupt the ecosystem," said Harris. "They were sticklers for making everything sustainable. Plus it doesn't disrupt krill-spawning habits."

"Jolly said there were more krill kollectors, though," Sam said. "It was like she disassembled lots of them to make a bigger one."

"There's plenty more. Rogers Ketchup is the worldwide leader in the tomato-based dipping-sauce game," Harris said. "My dad and his friends love that expensive stuff."

"But the sharks—did your dad and his friends make these sharks?"

"Pretty much, yes. There's a fleet of those things. I helped with the controls—I should know."

"So you did help her!" Neil accused.

Harris looked around the roof. "Neil, I did, but it's complicated. Can we go inside? I just got home, and I kinda need to pee. Plus we should seek shelter. The ostriches use this runway as a fight club in the evenings. It's awful."

Neil wasn't sure if he could fully trust Harris, but he'd had enough ostrich-related injuries for one lifetime, so he followed everyone back into Weo's office.

"Did you know anyone in Jolly's family?" asked Sam.

"Hmm. My dad does, maybe. Her family had some real pirates in it, though. From way back," Harris said. "My dad told me once to be nice to her, because practically her whole family has been killed by random shark attacks."

"Really?" said Neil.

"Her parents were boating, doing krill research," Harris said, his voice serious for once.

"Hence her plot for revenge," said Biggs.

"I really felt for her, so I did a little pro bono designing. Made the controls like a game," Harris. "Some of my best work, really. She said it was for science, so I didn't charge. Something about an aquarium she was opening up."

"Dude, that was the game at RebootCon. The one onstage with the sharks?" Biggs said. "Like, the biggest game that was demoed there. And you did it for free?!"

Harris raised his eyebrows.

"Oooh, that makes sense now," said Harris. "I thought that looked familiar. I was too busy with those glitches in Feather Duster. I never saw the demo."

"Well, it sounds like she stole your krill collector operating system to make her game, to find somebody to drive her evil shark," said Sam.

"Was the game fun?"

Neil stared blankly at Harris. He realized that his friend was innocent of any conspiring with Jolly. Harris was brilliant, but sometimes he totally didn't get it.

"Oh, it was a real hoot," said Neil sarcastically. "And news flash: I don't think that aquarium is real."

"So it's not an aquarium?" asked Harris.

"No way. She's made a monster to capture every living shark," Biggs said. "She wants to get rid of them all. Like they did her family."

"Wow, that seems a little intense," said Harris.

"So was your crazy scheme to take over the world," said Sam.

"Good point," Harris admitted. "Well, what can I do to help? I might have a copy of those game controls around here somewhere. Trevor kept asking me to try to get an advance copy of the game for him."

"Trevor?" Neil was intrigued.

"Yeah, when you guys left, I interfered with security so that no one got kicked out. It was pretty nice of them," said Harris, reaching into a dish of ostrich-shaped candies. He crunched them in his mouth, unaware that he'd witnessed Jolly's plan to select the best pilots to steer her megalodon.

"We've got to find everyone," Neil said firmly. "Before she does."

"Who is everyone? You mean the other nine of us?" Neil nodded.

"Something tells me she's not giving up just because we broke her shark's fin. She has a fleet of them, anyway," he said. "Plus she's going to go after more people to pilot that thing."

"So she's coming back for you guys?" asked Harris.

"Us, or the next best gamers alive, which would be our friends," said Sam.

"Harris, we're the only ones who know what's going on. The only ones who can stop Jolly," Neil said. "We need your help."

Harris finished crunching one last ostrich candy.

"Well, if we've got to do something, then let's do something," the boy billionaire said. He wasn't an evil villain after all, really.

"Harris, I'm gonna name a cat after you!" exclaimed Biggs. He ran to Harris and wrapped him in his wiry arms. "So what . . . do we do?"

"We're getting the team back together," Neil said. "We're coming out of retirement."

"Wait, we were retired?" said Biggs. "I thought it was just sort of an 'on pause' situation."

"Well, we're unpausing, then."

I just hope everyone else wants to.

Neil was still aware that his friends were probably furious that he'd ditched them at RebootCon.

"If we have to go find everybody, let's start making some calls," said Harris to the group. He glanced at his ever-present phone to look at the time. It read 2:33 in ostrich-shaped letters.

"Afraid we can't," said Weo. "I've been looking into it, and somebody's jamming signals in the area or something. For now, we're isolated."

Neil could hear the squawk of a few ostriches outside.

"Then we should split up," Harris said. "We can cover more ground separately, and it doesn't sound like we have much time to waste."

"How do you suggest we do that?" said Sam.

"Well, we've got my chauffeured jet here. Vinny's twin sister, Winnie, drives it. Sam, why don't you and Biggs go in there?" Harris said, pointing to the plane.

"And Neil and I, we'll pick up the other half of the group in my helicopter."

"Deal. We'll just take the helicopter," said Neil, trying his best to be cool. It wasn't as if he had any other modes of transportation to offer up. To his name, he owned a scooter he'd outgrown and a bike with two flat tires.

"The chopper's in the courtyard. I'll warm it up," Harris went on. "And since I only got my license a week ago, I'm calling dibs on Andertol as my copilot. No offense."

"None taken," said Biggs. "Does the jet have peanuts?"

"You'll find out soon enough. Neil, let's go. We might just have to battle a few ostriches first," Harris said.

"So it's settled. You get a few, we get a few, and we'll meet back here before sunset to stop Jolly. Easy."

Yeah, easy.

CHAPTER

15

NEIL AND HARRIS CLIMBED THE BRICK STAIRS THAT LED TO Corinne's front door. Next to the doorbell a sign read: EVERY TIME YOU PUSH THIS DOORBELL, A QUARTER IS DONATED TO PUBLIC RADIO.

The home itself was a charming cottage nestled into a small patch of pine trees. Neil pushed the doorbell and listened to the sound of a few chimes. After a minute the door was opened by a man Neil assumed was Corinne's father. He looked confused.

"Hi, hello, sir," Neil stammered. "I was wondering if Corinne might be home."

"Who might I tell her is here?" said Corinne's father. He was a stout African American man with trim hair and a gray mustache. He wore a tan suit coat with brown patches on the elbows and had a newspaper curled under his left arm.

"My name is Neil Andertol."

"Oh, Corinne," her father called out. "A Neanderthal boy is here to see you."

Really?

Her father unfolded his newspaper as he walked them toward the small kitchen. After a moment Corinne appeared in the doorway. She wore flannel pants and a baggy BEE CHAMPION T-shirt. Shocked to see Neil and Harris, Corinne ushered them to the living room.

"What do you want?" Corinne said. "Do you need help moving onto Reboot's yacht?"

"OK, I deserve that," Neil said. "And I'm really sorry. I wasn't thinking clearly, and I let the idea of meeting Reboot get the best of me."

"You can apologize all you want, but I used all my allowance money for three years to go on that trip," Corinne said. "And I barely spent time with everyone."

"Well, the good news is that we're getting everyone back together," Neil said. "Another mission."

Corinne's eyes lit up. She looked at her father, whose attention was on his paper's crossword puzzle. She sat down on the bench by her glossy upright piano. She crossed her arms and leaned back on the off-white keys. An ominous tone played, startling a cat sleeping in a nearby window.

"We need your help," Neil whispered. "That game at RebootCon wasn't a *game*. The creator was just finding people to use to capture sharks. Every shark."

"He's telling the truth, as crazy as it sounds," Harris added. A clock chimed in another room of the house. "Plus I'll give you five thousand Beed Airlines miles. You can go wherever you'd like."

Corinne wriggled her nose.

"Well, OK," said Corrine. "But you'll have to get this approved by my father somehow."

"Whatever that means, sure," Neil said.

"He'll demand one thing."

"What? A kidney? A spleen?"

"A spell-off."

"Right now?" Neil asked.

"*Y-E-S*," Corinne spelled out, cracking her knuckles to warm up.

"OK then," Neil said. "A spell-off it is."

"Dad, come here, please. Neil would like to speak with you."

★ ★ ★

SAM AND BIGGS HUDDLED ON THE GROUND, SURROUNDED by the vibrant colors of freshly fallen Montana leaves. Dried twigs crunched under their bodies as they crawled behind a fallen maple tree.

Phwap! Phwap!

Blue paint splattered just above their heads.

"Guys, do we really have to do this?" yelled Sam from behind a bulky safety mask.

"Sundays are for paintball! Nothing else!" yelled Dale. Bits of bark fell on Biggs's head as more paintballs peppered their tree bunker.

"But we need your help!" said Biggs, his hair dusted with tiny blue paint blobs.

"If you guys want us to help so badly, you'll have to earn it," said Dale from behind a giant spruce tree.

"I'd love to play all day, but we don't have time," said Sam, keeping her head tucked behind the makeshift bunker. "A lunatic ketchup pirate is threatening to kill every shark on the planet."

"With her own monster shark," Biggs said, poking his head up before a splash of orange paint tagged his curly hair.

The volley of paintballs stopped as Biggs heard the two boys step out from behind their shelter. A few birds chirped from hidden nests in the thick branches above.

"Did you say monster shark?" asked Waffles.

Biggs stood up, his clothes covered in new splotches of wet paint. Sam joined him, her hair now a neon blue.

"Monster *metal* shark, my dudes," said Biggs.

"Well, in that case, we're on board," said Waffles, lowering his bright-orange paintball gun. "Sundays are for paintball *and* sharks."

★　★　★

AS THE ENGINES LOWERED HARRIS BEED'S PRIVATE JET onto a field, people in capes and chain mail scattered in all directions.

"Lo, what metal bird is this?" shouted a villager, spilling the heavy bucket of cream he'd been carrying. "Get thee to thine horses!"

The plane had landed in the center of the Renaissance

fair, Riley's home away from home. Once again, he had found himself in the stocks. His stubby arms and head poked between wooden slats in the center of the town.

"Riley!" yelled Sam, stepping out from the jet and running toward him.

"Look how the flying woman moves just like one of us," said a frightened villager, never once dropping character. "What be this wizardry you share with us, magicke woman?"

"Ye olde jet plane," Sam said, popping the lock of Riley's stocks with a bobby pin. "Give it another hundred or so years; you guys will love 'em."

"While I appreciate this rescue, my fair compatriots," said Riley, "I'm not sure why 'tis happening."

"We've got a mission to complete!" yelled Biggs over the whirring of the jet engine.

"A mission? But whither is Jones?"

"Our own mission," said Sam. "We've got to find everyone else and put a stop to a crazy homeschooled pirate."

"Pirates?" said Riley. Other villagers shuddered at the very mention.

"Scallywags! If 'tis pirates you battle, then you will have my help," Riley exclaimed. "Onward, my friends!"

- -

"Agreed! Whatever all that meant, I agree!" yelled Biggs.

The citizens of the fake historical village continued to scream in terror as Riley was freed. Rubbing his wrists and neck, he walked after Sam toward the aircraft.

"Huzzah!" shouted Riley. "Send a pigeon to my mother; let her know I will return before the school bus cometh!"

The crew strapped into the safety harnesses of the plane and flew toward the San Diego airport, looking to retrieve Yuri and the Jasons.

"I hope there's still time," said Sam.

CHAPTER

16

"*I . . . S . . . T . . . H,* UH, *M . . . ,*" SAID NEIL, HIS EYES FIXED ON the ceiling above. "Can you use it in a sentence again?" he asked Corinne's father.

Neil's pulse pounded. Not only from the pressure of his first ever spelling bee, but from knowing that every passing second left another shark in danger. And once the sharks were gone, what would stop Jolly from going after anyone else who wronged her—animal or human?

"'Isthmus,'" said Corinne's dad. He was seated on the beige living-room couch with a huge dictionary resting on his stomach. He drank a small glass of rice milk, which left traces in his fuzzy mustache.

"The volunteer fireman found a pony on the isthmus."

What? Is that a sentence that someone has ever said in real life?

"Well, OK, 'isthmus,'" Neil shrugged. "*I-S-T-H-M-U-S*. 'Isthmus.'"

"That is correct," said Corinne's father. "Now on to round fifty-seven. Corinne, your word is 'adrenaline.'"

"Corinne, Father of Corinne, I hate to be rude, and believe me I would love to sit around here and spell and drink rice milk with your dad," Neil said, getting a glare from the spelling bee's judge, emcee, and timekeeper. "But we really need to go. I know I'm never gonna beat you in spelling anything."

"That's true," said the former spelling bee champion. She looked at Neil, then at her stern father. "If you really need my help, let's go. We're a team, right?"

Neil smiled, "We're a team! *T-E-A-M*."

She and Neil celebrated with a salute. Her father cleared his throat.

"I've never seen someone last so long in a heads-up spell-off with my Corinne. Nicely done, Neil."

Neil scratched the back of his head sheepishly.

"Nobody can beat your daughter, sir," Neil said. "To be honest, I was guessing on most of those."

"OK, Dad, I'll be back before curfew," said Corinne to her father. She quickly tied her shoes and zipped up a thin blue jacket.

"Now where was it you kids were going?" said Corinne's father, looking over the opened dictionary. Corinne gave him a kiss on the cheek.

"Oh, just to study," she said as the group skipped outside. "Be back soon!"

★　★　★

THE LATE-AFTERNOON SUN WAS TURNING THE SKY A LIGHT orange as Harris's helicopter touched down in a cul-de-sac of a residential neighborhood. Tall evergreens shook as the rotor blades slowed their spinning.

"You two go get our man," said Harris. "I'll stay here and watch the bird. If somebody puts a dent in this thing, my dad will take away international travel privileges."

Neil laughed and quickly unbuckled his safety harness.

"And try and get ahold of someone. The White House, Jones, anybody who might help."

Neil and Corinne ran out from the helicopter, hunched over as they headed toward the open door of a light-blue garage.

It was JP's, and he was inside, standing over a long table. It filled the space designated for two cars and was littered with random pieces of electrical wiring, several computers, and countless notepads filled with scribbled calculations. It was like a mad scientist's laboratory.

JP was hard at work on his science-fair magnets but looked up as Neil knocked on the frame of the open garage door.

"JP!" panted Neil. "We need you."

The boy genius was quiet.

"Oh, really? You don't say," JP answered. He had a small tray in his hands. It carried a few large potatoes. Yellow and blue wires curled out from the spuds. "You definitely didn't need me when you skipped out yesterday."

"That's totally fair that you're angry, and I'm sorry," Neil said. "But right now we truly need your help."

"I can't help you. I have to win the science fair," JP said proudly. "This week is nationals, Neil. The best presentation wins a scholarship. I have to dedicate every moment I have to this."

"JP, I'm begging you," Neil said.

"You can't leave a team to go to a yacht, just to come back in and flash a smile and win everyone over, Neil," JP said sternly. "Even if someone told you to do it. That's not being a good friend."

Neil let out a defeated sigh. They'd have to return to meet everyone without JP.

"JP, you have to trust him," said Corinne. "We need you. Every shark in the world could use your help."

JP looked puzzled.

"What's that?"

"We need your smarts," said Neil. "There's a lunatic with a metal shark roaming the oceans right now, ready to change life as we know it."

"Hmm, like that game?" JP said. He continued to tweak the wires connected to tiny silver disks. "From RebootCon?"

"Exactly."

"Even so, I can't leave—these magnets have been my life for months," JP said. "Today I had a breakthrough with the directional technology. I can pinpoint any magnetic metal up to five hundred yards away."

"Magnets are magic," said Neil. "I get that."

"Right? Aren't they exciting?"

It was becoming clear JP wouldn't be interested in anything nonmagnetic.

"So show me. Target . . . the helicopter rotor blades," Neil said, pointing to the aircraft outside.

"Yeah!" added Corinne. "Your project's already good enough to win, JP. I know it."

JP held up his potato display. "Behold."

After he plugged a few wires into the potatoes, the metal tray became a magnet. He leaned over his creation and pointed a metal disk at Harris and his chopper, aiming with his left eye. After flipping a small black switch, the magnet buzzed to life with a high-pitched ringing. After a second, the metal blades atop Harris's helicopter began to spin.

"Wow, that's awesome!" said Corinne.

"Thanks," JP said, a happy grin on his face.

"Well, good luck in the science fair, I guess," said Neil. "Let's go, Corinne. We've got to get back."

Neil and Corinne began walking down the smooth blacktop of JP's driveway.

"Wait," said JP.

Neil and Corinne turned to see their friend leaving

his garage laboratory, carrying a red duffel bag full of his experiments.

"I can call this experimenting in the field," JP said. "I'm always there for you guys. We've got sharks to save."

Neil was beginning to feel like a hero once again.

"What took so long?" said Harris when they got back to the helicopter. "I called the White House three times. Got a message they're closed on Sundays. Looks like we're on our own."

Sounds good to me. We can do this.

★ ★ ★

NEIL WAS THE LAST TO STEP OUT OF THE HELICOPTER AND back onto Harris's island. The four friends dodged ostriches as they walked to Weo's office.

On the ride over, Neil had made a satellite call to his mother, claiming he was getting a sneak peek at Reboot Robiskie's latest helicopter-themed game. Surprisingly, she'd already talked to Biggs's mom, who had filled her in about the gracious offer from the Robiskie Foundation and that they'd been given the VIP treatment. Neil's mom seemed worry-free about Neil's arrival and was looking forward to seeing Biggs's mom at this year's Quinoa and Gluten-Free Summit.

- -

"Back up and running?" Neil asked Weo.

The rest of the team joined Corinne, JP, and Neil in Weo's office. His desk was in disarray, covered in wires as he attempted to fix the phones and the internet connection.

"Not yet," Weo said. Neil looked around at his friends. But as he counted everyone, he saw there were only nine of them. Eleven with Weo and Harris. Either way, they were still short.

"Wait, where are the Jasons? And Trevor?" Sam asked, the roar of engines finally dying down.

"We thought you guys picked them up. Weren't they stranded at the airport?" said Harris.

"We thought you guys picked them up!" replied Biggs.

Neil felt a pit in his stomach. He knew there was only one person responsible for his missing friends—Jolly Rogers the Third.

CHAPTER 17

"SO TREVOR AND THE JASONS ARE JUST MISSING?" SHOUTED a panicked Yuri. "I was at that airport. I thought they got home." He leaned forward in a leather office chair.

"I wouldn't say they're missing," Neil explained. "More that they've been taken by a madwoman, and she's probably making them do her evil bidding."

"That's reassuring," said Yuri. The whole crew looked at Neil expectantly.

"So tell us, who is this girl again?" asked Corinne.

"Her name is Jolly Rogers," Neil said.

"The Third," added Sam.

"She created that shark game we played at the convention," said Neil. "Or at least kind of. She made Harris and other people build it for her."

The convention—wow, that seems so long ago.

"OK, what else? We were promised metal sharks," said Waffles. He wore his favorite camouflage bandanna, and still had splotches of paint on his left cheek.

"What?" said Riley. "Metal fish, Sir Neil?"

"Pretty much, yeah," Neil said. He paused for a moment to begin his best Jones impression. "Jolly Rogers has created a shark-submarine monster, and she's using it to find every shark in every ocean."

"And whither once these sharks are netted?" asked Riley.

"Well, her plan is to ultimately capture them all. After that, I can't imagine she'll do anything good with them."

"Who would want to eliminate every shark?" asked Dale.

"Someone whose family has a long history of death by shark," said Sam.

"Yeah, that'll do it," said Dale.

"I'm sick of people like Jolly hating on sharks!" shouted Biggs. He didn't seem to be himself, constantly wringing his hands and cracking fewer and fewer jokes. Neil felt bad for his friend. He knew that for someone who loved Earth as much as Biggs did, the idea of wiping out a whole species had to be terrifying.

"After we left Reboot's yacht, Jolly kidnapped us to force us to do her dirty work," Neil continued.

"So she used you for your gaming skills?" asked JP.

"Exactly," Neil said. "Luckily, we escaped. We damaged her shark, *Magda*, but something tells me she's going to be harder to stop than that."

Yuri raised his hand, and Neil pointed to him.

"Was Reboot's yacht cool?" he asked timidly.

"Very," said Neil.

"Everybody come see me after the mission. I'll give you some of Reboot's candy," added Biggs.

The group put their hands in the middle of a circle and did a giant high five. They were ready.

When everyone had settled down, Neil continued, "Jolly's boat had some sophisticated technology, like the jet fighters we piloted," said Neil. "I'm sure everything is cloaked, but her big secret is that her family's ketchup drives sharks crazy. It's how she lures them to her, so we can hopefully just follow their trail."

"Yes!" Weo shouted. The group turned to face him.

"Sorry," the boy president said. "I've got a connection, is all."

"No, that's good," said Biggs.

"No calls, unfortunately. Only internet, and it's sketchy—I'm bouncing a signal off some satellites."

"Nice—that's a pro move," said Yuri.

"But . . . I think I've got some news that may be helpful. Did you just say ketchup?" said Weo.

"Yeah, krill ketchup," said Neil. "She said it works better than anything to attract sharks. It's a secret recipe. I think her great-grandparents stole it from somewhere in Japan, during their pirate days."

"What did you find, Weo?" asked Sam.

"I just got a breaking news story emailed to me," said Weo. "The headline today was 'ketchup.'"

"So?" said Waffles, who was walking around the office and playing with ostrich toys.

"It looks like today was the biggest ocean ketchup spill in over seventy years. Since the great Tomato Tsunami, whatever that was."

Neil stared at the computer screen. A red banner was stretched across the top of the screen announcing BREAK-ING NEWS. Weo pressed play and clicked the volume to its highest setting. The video struggled, moving in choppy spurts.

"Breaking news internationally from the high seas," a newscaster said, her voice a powerful monotone. "In our top story, several freighters leaving from Japan and carrying high-end ketchup have all crashed in the Pacific Ocean during a routine shipment, spilling thousands of gallons of ketchup."

Neil gasped. The video continued, pausing a moment to buffer.

"And later, we break the story on yet another reported mass shark migration. We'll have live interviews with fishermen in Hawaii as they describe the incredible sight of hundreds of the wild animals swimming past their boats."

The anchorwoman turned to a new camera angle, shuffling a few papers in her hands.

"And now more on the Japanese freighters. From our business insider report, the cargo of most ships was mainly bottles of a rare luxury ketchup."

The anchorwoman continued.

"Spills have been reported from every corner of the Pacific Ocean but seem to be centralized toward the southwestern United States area. We'll keep you updated with every piece of information, no matter how small or unimportant."

The video stopped, and another about a waterskiing hedgehog began to load. Biggs looked conflicted as Weo exited the video player.

"We have to stop her!" Corinne yelped.

"You guys think those spills are this Jolly person?" said Weo. "If so, our islands aren't too far from their location."

"I know they aren't. The ketchup makes sharks go crazy. Jolly will be headed right for them, scooping up as many sharks as she can," said Sam. "Or making somebody else do it."

"I think she kidnapped Trevor and the Jasons to drive the megalodon," said Neil.

Neil was worried about Trevor. Not only was he an efficient and skilled pilot, but he always seemed to be out to prove himself. Mixed with the fact that Jolly was probably offering him a fortune beyond his wildest dreams,

Neil understood that it was not an ideal situation.

"I wish I could say I had some kind of foolproof plan, but I don't," Neil said to the team. He felt like he should be giving a brave speech like Major General Jones would—but his mind was blank. "I know that there's nothing we as a team can't solve, even if we're not all together."

The group remained hushed. Getting back together was the easy part. Now they were facing Jolly Rogers, the real threat.

"Well, time's ticking," said Dale. "Let's do this."

Dale nodded to his brother, Waffles, who took down a brightly colored Feather Duster 3 poster from the wall. He laid it out on the desk, leaving its blank white side facing up.

"Operation Shark Salvage and Condiment Cleanup is now officially under way," said Waffles, who uncapped an ostrich-shaped marker from Weo's desk. "We've got to get our friends back."

He drew a tiny shark in the upper right corner.

"And stop Jolly and her shark before it's too late," added Biggs.

Neil put a hand on his friend's shoulder.

"Right," said Dale. "A good plan always starts with a list of assets."

"Copy that," said Waffles. Across the top of the page he wrote *Things We Have*, underlining it for good measure.

"So, what *do* we have?" said Dale.

"I have about three thousand stuffed ostrich toys," said Weo. "And an entire shipment of defective ostrich visors, if that helps."

Waffles wrote *Ostriches?*

"I have my science-fair project. Would magnets help?" JP said.

"Definitely," said Neil.

"I have about eight uneaten chicken nuggets from the airport food court," said Yuri. "And seven different kinds of role-playing game dice."

Waffles continued to add items to the list.

"Whilst my saber is being sharpened, I am without a weapon," said Riley. "But I am clothed in a skin of metal."

Waffles began to write but paused.

"Chain mail, my lords and ladies."

"We have our vests," said Waffles, gesturing to his

black puffy vest that was peppered with paint. "Tear resistant. Fashionable."

"Oh, and my lasso. Can't leave home without it," said Dale.

The list was getting longer, but it read more like the lost and found from Reboot Robiskie's convention.

"Let's find a way to call Jolly. There's got to be a way we can reason with her," said Biggs.

"Working on it," said Weo. Yuri stepped next to him to help survey the issue.

"Until then, let me add to the list. I've got an almost-empty packet of red Singapore goo," said Biggs. Waffles slowly printed out the word "goo?"

"Wait," said Neil. He focused on a spot on the floor, processing something in his head.

"What is it?" asked Sam.

"Robot poodle."

"Is that like a comic book? Or a superhero I'm unaware of?" asked Waffles, pausing his marker before continuing with the addition.

"None of those things—just your old-fashioned real robot poodle," Neil said. "I met a girl named Marla at a science fair thing a while ago who was supposed to win a meeting with Reboot Robiskie. Instead, I have a hunch Jolly hijacked her prize-winning invention. She's been getting kids to do everything for her."

"And you have it on you?" asked Yuri, looking at Neil's normal-looking pants pockets.

"No, Jolly has it. But I bet I know exactly where it is," Neil answered. "And it has the ability to disable any electronics in the area."

"Robot poodle!" Waffles shouted, writing it down.

"Maybe we can try to stop the sharks from getting eaten," said Biggs. "Like dilute that ketchup or something."

"Nothing a few thousand ostrich toys can't suck up," said Weo.

Neil was getting excited. This was beginning to sound like, well, a plan.

"There's just one little problem, guys," said Harris. "The boat's getting a tune-up. And we can't fly a jet to a spot in the ocean."

"Um, helicopter?" said Sam, pointing toward the machine outside. On the poster Waffles wrote *CHOPPER!!!*

"I don't know if we'll be able to get far," Harris said.

"We used up a good amount of fuel, and our next ship-ment doesn't get in for a few days."

The group hushed, deep in thought.

"We're in luck," said Neil with a proud smile. "We've got a guy."

CHAPTER 18

"I DIDDDONN'T KNOW BOATTTS WENT THISSSS FASSSTTT." Neil yelled to Reboot Robiskie. Reboot sat at the helm of his yacht in his uniform of loose-fitting linen. Despite their tremendous speed, his sunglasses stayed firmly planted on the top of his head.

Neil occupied the chair next to him, while most of his friends were wedged into the couches on the ship's lower decks. They shared a look of shock that they were actually on Reboot's yacht. Candy would have to wait for later, unfortunately.

"WeoOOo, do you co-py-py?" said Neil in a radio receiver.

"Roger that, Neil," said Weo. He'd offered to stay at the warehouse, serving as the team's home base. He'd been able to send a message to Reboot through his site's servers, and now they were talking through the high-tech radios on Reboot's ship. None of his technology had been affected by whatever Jolly had done.

"Ten-fourrrrr," clacked Neil. He studied the endless ocean as the boat headed east. The night was settling, and bright stars began to glow overhead.

"Do you know Jololololly?" Corinne asked Reboot, who sat on Neil's other side.

Reboot shook his head no and continued to focus on the water ahead. He'd turned off his outboard lights to cruise in total darkness.

Jolly still had no clue they were coming for her. Using coordinates that Weo had estimated from the ketchup spill, plus Reboot's cloaking technology, the team was hoping for a surprise visit.

"Straight ahead," said Reboot. He craned his neck forward, looking into the open water.

"What is it?" Neil asked as the boat began to slow.

He figured they must've been going a million knots per hour, minimum.

Ahead of the boat, Neil could see the nose of a capsized ship sticking out of the water. On its side was a picture of an animal Neil would never forget: a krill. Neil could see an endless stream of fins headed toward the damaged hull of the boat.

"That thing's gonna bring a million sharks right to it," said Neil.

The radio in Neil's hand began to crackle to life.

"What was that, Weo? Static on my end."

The radio popped a few times more before a voice came through clearly.

"Good evening, Neil," it said. It was certainly not Weo, but rather the shrill voice of Jolly Rogers the Third.

"You'll be interested to know the first one thousand sharks have been deposited at the new Rogers Ketchup processing facility," she said. "And we're just getting started."

Neil's stomach twisted.

"Trevor, can you hear me?" screamed Neil into the radio. "Trevor, if you can, stop. You've got to stop."

Neil could hear Jolly laugh, with the sound of her

caged birds squawking in the background.

"Oh, Neil, I think Trevor is quite happy here," she said. "He's become a better pilot than you. Looks like he just needed you out of the way."

"Easy," said Neil. "Trevor knows what we think of him."

"Yeah, and it's not much, from my understanding," said Jolly. "Trevor and all your Jasons work for me now."

Reboot cut the engines, allowing his ship to coast over the dark water.

"This radio broadcast tells me you may be getting a few ideas, Neil," Jolly continued. "I will be clear: You got lucky once before. It won't happen again. Don't do anything . . . stupid."

With a sizzle the radio went silent. Neil could hear his friends leaving the cabin below. Reboot looked at his top-of-the-line radar equipment, then pointed to the starboard side of the boat with two fingers.

"The shark."

He could see the slightly crooked dorsal fin of *Magda* slowly break the surface. It rose ten feet out of the water, almost taunting Neil. Neil could see the fin had been reattached—affixed by huge strips of metal.

"Wow, she fixed it," said Neil. "That fin has to be weakened. If we can tear it off once more, we'd send *Magda* spinning."

"With our friends inside, though," said Corinne.

"Well, we got out in an emergency escape pod," Neil said. "There's hopefully another."

Hopefully.

"We can work on the shark. You need to get on that ship," said Reboot.

He watched the huge fin of *Magda* dip below the water's surface, then return again.

Where was Jolly's yacht?

If they could find her ship, they would certainly find Jolly—she would never leave her fancy yacht now that she'd set her plan in motion.

"Reboot, do you see anything on the radar? Like another ship?" asked Neil.

He studied the green screen of the radar system, watching each pulse as it located nearby objects.

"Doesn't look like anything," Reboot said. "But let me try something else. With invisibility technology what it is, we've gotta stay one step ahead of everybody."

Oh, believe me, I know.

"There you are," said Reboot at the screen. Neil peered over to see the outline of Jolly's unconventional-looking ship. "She must have some sort of active camouflage. Her shark's still cruising around, though."

Reboot restarted the boat and made his way toward the blinking beacon.

Neil could see *Magda* swishing through packs of wriggling sharks. With a creak, its jaws opened wide. A school of sharks was sucked into the holding tank of its stomach. Neil shuddered to think of how many it had already captured.

"I'll get you to her boat," said Reboot, who was still in his comfy white captain's chair. "Then we can work on getting these sharks out of here."

Suddenly, Jolly's yacht was visible no more than fifty yards ahead.

"Heads up, two people on guard," whispered Corinne.

Pierre and Fabien sat on either side of Jolly's ship. They carried huge spotlights, along with big metal crossbows.

"This will have to be quick," said Reboot softly, studying the ship ahead. The bubble of invisibility was large, probably enough to give *Magda* freedom to roam before depositing its most recent shark payload. "I'm not sure if we can get close undetected."

"I wish you could just swim there—that'd be easiest," said Corinne.

"Right, swim through an ocean of sharks," said Neil. "That should go well."

He paused to think about Jolly's boat itself.

"That's not half bad, though. What if we just went through them?" said Neil. "Jolly's boat is pretty weird. It's two pontoons with a fancy dining room connecting them. There's space to drive through."

Reboot's eyes narrowed.

"They'd hear and see our ship. It has to be totally silent," he said. "We could use the small emergency ship we've got, but even then that'd be too loud. And you'd have to be crazy to just have a piece of plastic between you and sharks."

Neil smiled. For his friends, and animals everywhere, he knew he would have to be that crazy.

"Waffles!"

The boy appeared from the deck below, his lips covered in a large amount of Singapore goo.

"We still have that list?"

Waffles nodded and ducked back inside. He returned with a rolled-up ostrich poster.

"Reboot, Wifi, let's get that plastic boat."

★ ★ ★

"MUSTARD ME, PEOPLE," NEIL SAID.

Neil twirled in a circle as his friends, along with Reboot, splattered him with a variety of mustard taken from all across the globe. Having a well-stocked fridge was coming in handy.

"All right, everybody, I think that's good," Neil said to his team, spitting yellow glop from his mouth. "I hope this even works. . . ."

"Just to be safe," said Waffles, squirting a bit more mustard for good measure. "And don't worry, this logic holds up. If the sharks love this ketchup, they'll hate mustard. I know it."

"I just wouldn't fall in," said Wifi Whitner, who was with the crew downstairs.

Neil got into the same tiny raft that had dropped him off outside Biggs's house. He looked toward his destination. Even from far away, Jolly's yacht looked much bigger than he remembered.

JP cautiously stepped onto the small boat, lugging potatoes from Reboot's kitchen. He secured them at the front of the craft, quickly plugging in the blue spiral wires of his magnets. He leaned down and aimed the magnet's pull toward a corner of Jolly's boat.

"These will be strong enough to pull you toward her ship," explained JP. "No motor. No sound." He gave Neil a salute and climbed back aboard Reboot's ship.

Neil wore Dale's paintball vest, which was then covered with Riley's chain mail. All of it was now dripping with pungent yellowish mustard, as it was decided by the group that it was the best shark repellent.

He turned back to his friends, who were on the deck. "You guys try to soak up that ketchup," he said. "I'll take care of Jolly and *Magda*."

"And remember to let the wrist do the work," yelled Dale, making a lasso motion. Neil looked at the lasso in his hands. When he was close enough, he'd rope himself in to Jolly's ship and quietly sneak aboard. Well, as quietly as one could wearing chain mail dipped in hot dog toppings.

"I'll radio once I've stopped her," Neil said. "Good luck, guys—we can do this."

"Aye, aye, Captain Andertol," said Biggs with a salute. He gave Neil a push, giving him distance from Reboot's ship.

With a tiny buzz the magnets came to life, and Neil was jerked toward Jolly and her henchmen. As the moon shone on the water, Neil could see and hear sharks in every direction. His heart pounded as he felt them bump into his boat.

"OK, my hungry friends, I'm here to help you. Let's be cool," Neil said. "And if I make it out of this, I promise to eat only mustard sandwiches from here on out."

CHAPTER

19

PIERRE AND FABIEN WERE POSTED ON THE TOP OF JOLLY'S ship, shining spotlights out into the sea's rolling waves. Neil knew he would be done for with a single arrow from one of their crossbows. He lay flat on the floor of the boat, his face inches from the mouths of ketchup-hungry sharks.

Click.

Neil felt the raft stop moving. He lifted his head to see JP's magnets had connected with the sparkly paint job of Jolly's boat.

"Here goes nothing," Neil murmured to himself. He tossed Waffles's lasso up, but he didn't allow enough slack. The looped end hit the side of the boat and splashed into the water. Neil ducked down and hoped Jolly's henchmen hadn't heard.

Neil gathered the lasso once more. With a flick of his wrist, he managed to wrap the rope around the thin metal handrail above. Neil gave enough slack for the looped end to fall down to him. He fished the other end of the rope through the lasso and pulled the rope tight so that it slid up and made a knot around the handrail.

As Neil tugged down on the rope, *Magda* resurfaced fifteen yards from him. He watched its eyes glow red under the shimmering water. More important, though, Neil felt his boat begin to be magnetically pulled toward the shark. It must've locked onto its fin.

"Yipes," said Neil as he grabbed tight to the rope. This would be his first rope climb since gym class, where he'd held on for ten seconds before dropping to a soft mat on the ground. Now, below him were sharks.

Neil's shoes squeaked as he planted them on the side of the boat. Slowly, he walked himself upward, gripping the rope with all his strength. He turned to see his boat chase after *Magda*, and watched Pierre's and Fabien's flashlights illuminate a splotch on the deck of the ship. Another splash of red goo fell from above.

Red goo on demand, and a repaired drone. This is the best day yet for Scones 'n' Drones.

Pierre and Fabien chased after the mysterious glop. They followed it to the front of the ship.

"Perfect distraction," Neil gasped, collecting himself.

He reached hand over hand up the frayed rope, finally throwing a leg over the top to fling himself up.

Neil's hands burned, as did his lungs. He lay on his back and looked at the sky above. He took a deep breath. The ship smelled like ketchup, fish, and, well, feet.

Now let's keep going.

With Jolly's guards on the other end of the ship, Neil rushed down one side. His shoes squeaked, so he did his best to walk on his toes. The sounds of thousands of thrashing sharks seemed to drown out other noises, so Neil raced to the stairway leading up to Jolly and took the stairs two at a time.

He tore open the glass door leading into Jolly's captain's quarters.

The interior of Jolly's ship was in disarray. Yellowed, old-looking books were thrown to the floor. The lace drapes above the windows were torn.

"Fancy seeing you here," said Jolly. She was hunched over the huge birdcage—its doors were open. She fed the albino birds pellets from her hand.

"Jolly," said Neil calmly. "Where are my friends?"

His eyes scanned the contents of her lavish cabin. Neil noticed just how many collectibles she really did have.

"Oh, I think you know quite well where they are," she said, examining his outfit. "And—you're staining the carpet! You mustard freak!"

Neil kept his attention on the shelves full of valuables. *Each one of these is probably stolen from a kid genius. Especially that poodle!*

Neil's eyes focused on Marla's invention. It was next to a mask with bright feathers and a fake red bird.

Neil leaped at the toy dog.

Jolly looked startled but didn't stop him. He turned Marla's poodle on and pushed a button. He watched the small dog do a flip, then bark.

"Yes!" Neil cheered. He aimed the dog outside,

toward the metal shark passing through a sea of fins. It barked once more.

Nothing happened.

Jolly howled with laughter. She pressed a control in her hand, and Neil saw *Magda* pop out of the water, scooping in a new mouthful of victims.

"Oh, Neil," Jolly laughed. "There's no help for you here. But I thank you for coming back to watch me finish what you started."

Neil pushed the buttons on the back of Marla's robot poodle, but it just kept barking. He could hear the jaws of *Magda* slam shut even through the thick glass.

Why did I think that would work?

"I just fancied that thing as a toy," Jolly said, pacing around her cabin. She dragged a finger along a crushed velvet drape. The boat rocked as the megalodon rushed past. "I've got governments and corporations bending over backward to help me. I go poaching ideas from young minds for fun. Nobody bats an eye if you make kids do everything for you, as long as you give them a free game or pizza."

"Jolly, you've got to stop while you still can," Neil argued, chucking the poodle to the ground. "It's not too late."

"Oh, there's no stopping now," she said through gritted teeth. "Those jaws are eating everything in sight. And you're next, Neil Andertol."

Jolly lunged at Neil, her eyes furious. The two crashed into a small table that held a tea set that must've been two hundred years old. It shattered as Jolly tackled Neil. She pinned him down, driving her knees into his elbows.

Her hair was a mess, and her eyes were red. She'd had either too little sleep, too much Singaporean candy, or both.

"Jolly, you could use that robot shark for so much good, instead of evil," Neil said. "What if you helped sick sharks or something? Instead of killing them?"

"Help? Sharks ruined my life," Jolly yelled. "They made me live on a boat and have nothing but two hairy men for a family."

"That is a rough deal, I agree," said Neil. "But sharks are misunderstood. Like you and me."

"You?"

"Yeah, you bet. I'm still trying to get people to call me 'Neil' at school."

"What?"

"That's not important," Neil continued. He heard one

of Jolly's birds squawk. They were perched right above him on a windowsill. "But school is pretty rough, is what I'm saying. So is being a high-seas orphan, I'd imagine."

Neil tried to loosen her hold on him, but she was strong. She even got a hand free to remotely open and close the mouth of her shark, sucking in more sharks. Neil noticed she was pushing another button—probably sending shocks right through his friends.

"But Jolly, when school is unfair, I don't round up every kid who's mean to me with a giant metal shark."

"Are you practicing a speech right now?" said Jolly with a disgusted face. "I can do whatever I want! I wish you had just helped me like I asked, Neil."

"I am helping you. You've got to cut this out! I can tell you're a smart person."

Neil heard a voice on Jolly's radio.

"Captain."

It was Pierre or Fabien. "We have spotted zem. A boat—zey've been trying to run over ze shark fin. Permission to take zem down."

The captain struggled to keep Neil pinned and press the transmission for her radio. She pushed the radio's button with the back of her hand.

"Granted," said Jolly, speaking slowly as if to enjoy each syllable.

While she was still transmitting to Fabien and Pierre, Neil did his best Jolly impression.

"And *Magda*'s emergency capsule? Installed?" he said, impressing himself with an accent that wasn't too over-the-top.

Jolly glared down at him as Neil violently squirmed, shaking the radio to the ground beside them.

The men simply responded, "*Oui*." That meant a safe escape for Trevor and the Jasons.

"You're toast, Neil," Jolly fumed. But for a second she eased her hold on Neil. He grabbed the bottom of a long iron lamp that was next to him. With all his strength, he flung it at the window.

Its pointed and intricate design worked perfectly to shatter the glass into millions of pieces. Bewildered, or possibly sensing freedom, her albino parrots flapped their way out into the warm night.

"No! No!" Jolly shrieked. She ran to the window. "My beloveds! How dare you, you monster!"

Neil raced to the other side of the cabin with the radio.

"Ohhh, Jolly," Neil said, his eyes glowing with an

idea. He made his way to the control deck. "If you're not going to stop this, I will."

"If you're looking to take over my *Magda*, I'll have you know the only controls are right here," Jolly said, leaning out of her cabin. She was flourishing a tiny remote in her hand. "Can't trust you not to break anything."

"Nope, you can't."

I hope this works.

Neil reached the controls for the boat and pulled the lever for the anchor, dropping it toward the ocean floor far below. He could hear the splash of the heavy hook as it hit the water, and the metal sounds of chains unspooling.

But Neil stopped it before it made contact. As he jerked the lever back up, it snapped in half.

Now Jolly would have no way of pulling the few hundred feet of chain and giant metal anchor back up. Neil yelled into the radio he'd taken from Jolly.

"Trevor! I know you're not an actually evil person, so you've got to help me stop this crazy pirate. You're the hero for this mission."

Neil heard no response.

"Even if she starts electrocuting you, you've got to

bring her down," Neil said. "The anchor—I need you to bite the anchor and sink her ship. It's the only chance to stop her."

There was nothing again. Neil wasn't sure if he had broken the radio, too, but he had to trust that his message was getting to Trevor. "It's time to go deep-sea fishing."

As Neil tossed the radio on the captain's chair, Jolly appeared at the controls. She carried a heavy, pointy candelabra in her hands.

"Neil, I have to finish this," Jolly said. She swung the long piece of metal toward Neil.

"Why?"

"For my family. To get their revenge."

Neil felt truly sorry for her.

"Jolly, revenge isn't the way to do that," Neil said. "Your family probably wants you to keep making ketchup."

"I don't care about ketchup!"

"Well, that's fine," Neil said. "There are lots of things other than ketchup and shark vengeance. But if you want to keep being rich, I bet you'll want to keep the oceans safe. You're getting rid of what your family loved by destroying something you alone hate."

- -

Skrrkkk.

"What's that?" said Jolly. The boat jerked, and she and Neil both grabbed the captain's chair to stabilize themselves.

"Trevor!"

He's actually not evil after all. I knew it all along, mostly.

Bubbles rose to the surface of the water as the ship was tugged straight down by the power of *Magda*. With a groan, the boat started to give in to the force, its shiny exterior beginning to bend and snap.

"Oh, no!" yelled Jolly, clutching a railing on the side of her cabin. They were slowly sucked down toward the water and the sharks. With each passing second, the stern of the ship rose out of the water as the middle of the ship buckled in. The deck creaked, and Neil could hear water rushing into Jolly's fancy cabin. Her doilies and plush rugs were most definitely soaked.

He grabbed the radio from Jolly's captain's chair.

"Reboot! Time to come pick me up!"

As the ship lurched down again, Neil clipped the radio to the neck of his chain mail and made his way to the deck. Sharks of all sizes still swam, though there seemed to be less ketchup spurring them on.

The boat began to sink, and sink fast. The water was

fifteen feet away, and getting closer with each passing second. Neil could hear *Magda* churning underwater, struggling against the buoyancy of the large boat.

"Jolly!" shouted Neil.

She didn't look at him.

"Jolly!"

Again, nothing. She seemed defeated, as if she'd given up. Water splashed all around her, washing over her in thin sheets.

From Neil's right, though, came a flash of light. He looked to see Reboot's boat, its lights and engine now fully on. Neil waved his arm as someone put a spotlight on the front of the ship.

"Neil! This thing's gonna blow; we're outta here!" came Trevor's voice. "Find us after so we can get medals!"

Neil could hear the sounds of his friends scrambling toward their escape pod. He heard the creak of metal doors, and soon a thousand captured sharks were set free back into the ocean. They swam away in every direction as the overheating *Magda* kept pulling Jolly's yacht toward the seafloor.

"Neil!" shouted Sam, leaning over the side of Reboot's ship. "Hop on!"

Reboot's boat edged closer, and Neil managed to crawl to the top deck of Jolly's ship. He balanced on slippery metal and jumped into the outstretched arms of Corinne and Sam. They fell backward, all landing with a thud from Neil's chain mail.

"Huzzah!" shouted Riley. "Lord Andertol returneth!"

Neil shimmied free from his mustard-metal tunic. He cupped his hands around his mouth to yell back to the girl clinging to a sinking boat.

"Jolly, you don't have to go down with your ship," yelled Neil.

"I do!" she yelled. "All great captains do!"

"You're not a great captain!" Neil replied. "You're actually an awful, evil captain. But now you just get to be Jolly Rogers the Third, landlubber."

The sharks greedily snapped at the half-broken bottles of ketchup floating on the ocean's surface.

"We already captured Pierre and Fabien," added Biggs, gesturing to Reboot's kitchen. "They were actually pretty OK with everything once they saw the amount of dark chocolate Reboot's got on this thing."

"Just get over here!" yelled Corinne.

The water churned below, even faster.

"But you all hate me. There's no way of changing that," Jolly said, watching her ship sink deeper and deeper.

"Don't say that," said Neil. "Just today everybody was mad at me for leaving them to see Reboot Robiskie."

"Yeah!" said Corinne. "And now everything's great. Except for the sharks."

Corinne looked right at Jolly. "People won't always hate you," she said. "But you have to work to make it that way, Jolly."

"You don't know the feeling of being alone like I do. None of you do," Jolly snarled.

"I highly doubt that," said Neil. "As alone as you think you are, somebody on this boat has you beat. We've got a guy who lives for cleaning up animal dung."

"I conversed only with pigs for an entire month last year," shouted Riley.

"And I know all about being homeschooled," yelled Corinne. "We're both just a couple of mixed-up girls getting taught stuff by father figures with facial hair. Come over here."

"What's the point? I've been running from boarding school. Once the authorities get me, I'll be sent away,"

Jolly confessed. "I'm supposed to be there now, but it's—inland. Landlocked. Disgusting."

The bow of the ship was nearly submerged. Jolly had walked out to the last part of the ship still above the water. Neil watched the red eyes of *Magda* turn off below.

"Being away from the ocean isn't so bad," said Neil. "Sure, there's more manure than you bargain for, but you'll get used to it. I thought I hated the ocean before this weekend; now I kind of like it."

Then came a noise Neil had heard before.

Cacaw!

After a few flutters, Jolly's two pet parrots landed on Neil's shoulders. They pecked at the bits of mustard in his ears.

"If . . . if I do," the girl said. Her voice was thin and afraid. "Promise me there aren't any actual pig droppings aboard."

"Promise," Neil said.

Reboot swung the boat back toward Jolly, and Neil extended his hand. Jolly took it and dropped the remote control to grab Neil's arm. "Hold on."

With Corinne's, Sam's, and Biggs's help, they yanked

Jolly away from her ship as it sank in a burst of bubbles.

"Neil, Neil!" came a voice from the radio. "Can you hear me, Neil? This is submarine Captain-for-Life Trevor Grunsten."

Neil smiled and unclipped the radio from the chain mail on the floor.

"Trevor, I—"

"Save it. That was a good speech back there," Trevor said. "I was trying to escape. It just . . . it is kinda hard to think when you keep getting electrocuted."

"Believe me, I know."

"This heroing is tough business," Trevor said. "Glad I was around to do it."

Neil rolled his eyes.

"Any good hero has to be humble—that's the first thing they teach you," Neil joked. "Now get back here safe and sound. We've got victory slushies to share."

Neil's radio was silent, then came back to life.

"Neil, we're sorry about the sharks," said Jason 1. "She said she had you three locked up somewhere. We didn't want to—"

"No worries, everybody," Neil said. "We're all OK now."

As Jolly coughed up a few gulps of water, the group's attention went to the weary captain. Her hair was wet and stringy, bouncy curls now matted to the sides of her almond-shaped face.

"I . . . I'm not sure what to say," Jolly mumbled.

"We'll start with an 'I'm sorry' and go from there," said Sam.

"And might I suggest playing a video game every now and then?" asked Corinne.

Jolly cackled.

As Neil looked at the water, it was finally free of shark fins, but the items from Jolly's ship littered the surface of the ocean. Her fancy leather-bound books and cheese plates now drifted through waves.

They watched Trevor and the Jasons guide their submarine safely toward Reboot's ship, while Biggs began preparing a giant sugar feast.

Neil walked over to the weary Captain Rogers and knelt down beside her.

"Sorry," she said. Her birds sat perched on each of her bony knees. He handed her a towel.

"Don't be," Neil answered. "We'll figure this out."

"The sharks haven't been killed yet, promise."

"I believe you," Neil said. "Now let me introduce you to my friend Reboot. I think you might find you have some things in common."

Neil and Jolly, both wrapped in fluffy towels, got up and walked toward the party.

"Did you say his name is 'Boot'?" Jolly asked before stepping inside. "Like a foot boot? I'm not too keen on other people's feet."

Neil stifled a laugh. "Jolly, we've got some work to do with you."

The door closed behind them as Neil spent a final night at sea—this time with all his friends, both new and old.

CHAPTER 20

NEIL ANDERTOL SLOWLY OPENED HIS EYES, GROGGY FROM blissful sleep. He'd been dreaming, a phenomenon he'd enjoyed as of late. His nightmares, which at one point were nonstop, seemed to have vanished.

"Time for karate, Neil Andertol!"

His sister, Janey, opened the magenta drapes covering the hotel room windows. The room overlooked the Pacific Ocean and the glowing morning sun, and he could see the former site of RebootCon farther south. Janey practiced her karate moves in front of a full-length mirror. She was still in her pajamas, but throwing phantom punches at a tournament-level pace.

"You think there's gonna be some possible mid-parade combat happening this morning?" Neil asked, turning toward his sister. The door connecting to their parents' room was open, and Neil heard the sounds of them getting ready to leave.

"I've got to be at the top of my game, Neil," said Janey. "The Karate Parade comes but once a year."

Janey had been invited to march in the San Diego Karate Parade. This first event of what everyone hoped would be a new tradition that filled the streets of San Diego with people in gis. Janey hadn't seemed too excited, but Neil had convinced her and the family it would make for a great trip. It also happened to fall on the opening week of Captain Jolly's Shark Adventure—San Diego's newest water-themed adventure park, conveniently located on the former site of a shark collection facility. Neil was more interested in the new park.

"How long does this parade thing last?" asked Neil, rummaging through his bag for a pair of shoes. "I really want to make the opening of that new park."

"It'll end when it ends. There's lots going on with

it," Janey said, folding her hands together before bowing to the long mirror. "We're trying to top the world record for most people breaking through wooden boards on a one-way street."

"Neil, your sister's parade will end by one," their mother said from her room. "For pushing so hard to come here, you should want it to last the whole day. You *are* still grounded when we get home, I'll have you remember."

"I know. I just *really* want to get to the shark adventure," Neil said. "I've, ah, read a lot about it. It sounds cool is all."

"And I just want to get to the Karate Parade!" shouted Janey, punching a cup of ballpoint pens from the hotel room's desk.

"Nose kicksing din the hotel phroom!" said Neil's mom, in the middle of brushing her teeth. Neil heard her turn the faucet on and spit. "OK, we're going. Before somebody breaks a window in here."

★ ★ ★

NEIL WALKED ALONE THROUGH THE TURNSTILE LEADING into Captain Jolly's Shark Adventure—a real aquarium after all. Families walked in fascination, taking in the cutting-edge tanks that covered every surface. Field trips of classes walked together, each kid wearing a set of head-phones for the educational tour.

Through a grant from Rogers Ketchup, Jolly had built a huge series of tunnels, all using glass that was inches thick. It allowed guests to feel like they were actu-ally underwater.

The tunnel system also allowed sharks and other sea life to come and go with ease, free to stay or leave at their leisure. Guests and sharks could enjoy ancient ketchups together. Plus there was funnel cake.

She turned her shark prison into a shark vacation.

With Neil's family busy at the parade, he roamed freely around the theme park. He waltzed through the hall of jellyfish and did his best to get an otter to wave at him.

Neil watched a father and daughter stare at a pack of hammerheads gliding a few feet beneath them. Even the floors were glass at Captain Jolly's Shark Adventure. Neil turned and headed for the far side of the building, his shoes squeaking.

"Captain Neil Andertol!" came a voice. Neil looked to see Captain Jolly Rogers the Third. She was smiling and cheerful, wearing a fresh all-white captain's outfit. CAPTAIN JOLLY was stitched in gold on the front pocket of her shirt. "Allow me to introduce you to the first ever swim-through shark observatory."

Neil gave Jolly a quick hug. He was really getting the hang of befriending former supervillains.

"Jolly, congratulations!" said Neil. "The place is unreal. I think the floors are cleaner than any plate I've eaten off in a year."

"Do you like it?" the sea captain asked eagerly. "I made this in my parents' honor. I found some of their old shark research and wanted to continue it."

"That's great, Jolly," Neil said.

"There's actually a marine biology club at my new boarding school. Who would've thought?" Jolly said.

"Fantastic."

"Reboot Robiskie has decided to help, too."

"Yeah, he mentioned that in his last letter," Neil said. "We're kind of pen pals."

Jolly smiled. "We've been helping nurse hurt sharks back to health. All of their own accord, of course. We're using *Magda* to locate sharks with life-threatening issues, but they're never held captive. We have an open-door policy. There's really no door at all, though, so I guess that doesn't make sense."

Neil laughed.

"Much better than the burlap bag policy I fondly remember."

The black walkie-talkie on Jolly's hip crackled. She pushed a button on the small white earpiece she wore in her left ear.

"Copy that," said Jolly. "I hate to run, Neil, but I unfortunately have more ribbons to cut and hands to shake."

"Definitely understood, and don't get those switched around," Neil joked. "I'll make sure to say good-bye."

Jolly handed Neil a stack of coupons. Each said ONE FREE HOT DOG in blue block letters.

"Lunch is on me," Jolly said. "And make sure to stop by the ketchup bar—I have a hunch you'll really enjoy it. Especially our more exotic flavors from across the globe."

"I'm actually more of a mustard man these days."

With a wink, Jolly slipped back into the crowds.

Neil's eyes drifted across the new adventure park. He felt proud—like he'd helped Jolly realize the good she was meant to do. He watched a powerful great white shark swim between the glass tunnels of humans. Neil walked to the concession stand and ordered his first free hot dog.

A few loud chimes drew the attention of the crowd. Neil stopped chewing and wiped some nonkrill mustard from his lips.

"Pardon me, friends, family, and anemones, but we have a special Jolly's World announcement," said the voice. "Today we have a guest of honor. Neil Andertol, please come to the Jolly Family Theater."

Guest of honor?

Neil finished his hot dog in a few quick bites, wiped his fingers on his pants, and ran toward the theater. An elderly usher in a bright-red coat stood outside, blocking the doorway with a velvet rope.

"Are you Neil?" the gray-haired woman said. Neil nodded yes and smiled. "Well then, enjoy."

Neil opened the large door leading into the theater.

Inside, he saw something he'd never expected.

WELCOME TO NEILANDERCON said a huge banner strung above the aquatic stage. The seats of the theater were all empty, but onstage was a maze of video-game booths, just like at the convention Neil had missed months before.

But instead of new games with countless assistants helping, it was staffed only by Neil's friends—new and old.

"If anybody deserves his own convention, it's you," said Sam. "And just to let you know, Reboot helped set it up."

Neil was speechless.

"Let the Great Neil Conference begin!" yelled Riley. He wore a sparkly new helmet and rust-colored chain mail. "Neil, perchance you fancy a game of Stable Clean? 'Tis the most realistic bovine waste-removal simulator ever made."

"You set it up and I will be there soon, my friend," said Neil.

In the next booth stood Trevor, wearing a white fencing outfit.

"And then you and I are digital fencing," Trevor said, sliding his metal mask to the top of his head. The two shook hands. Neil felt good knowing he could count on Trevor, even if he was difficult.

Neil looked at the rest of the convention. His smile hurt. This was like having seven surprise birthday parties at once. Weo manned a Feather Duster 3 booth, and even Pierre and Fabien hosted a game about making crepes.

"Neil!" yelled Waffles. He was covered in camouflage paint. "Come check this out."

He stood by Reboot Robiskie and Wifi Whitner, who were planted in one of the massive shark heads from Jolly's game.

"I'm . . . I'm not even sure what to say, guys," Neil stammered.

Jolly walked behind Neil, entering through the same doors he'd just used.

"Well, what do you think?" she asked, still wearing her same devilish smile.

"It's perfect. Thanks," Neil replied.

"No, thank *you*, Neil," Jolly said. "I mean it. All this wouldn't have happened without you. I now have friends, actual friends. People who won't do stuff for me if they don't want to."

Neil chuckled and watched his friends as they roamed the theater, playing games against one another.

"Now go enjoy your party, Neil Andertol," Jolly said, patting Neil's back. "You've earned it."

Neil nodded.

"Game on!"

ACKNOWLEDGMENTS

Deep thanks to my fantastic editors and cocaptains, Hayley Wagreich and Catherine Wallace. I also wish to thank the team at Alloy, including Josh Bank, Sara Shandler, Les Morgenstein, Joelle Hobeika, Romy Golan, and Heather David.

I am very grateful for the artistic minds that make Neil and friends look so stylish. Thanks to Alloy's Natalie Sousa, and to the art department at HarperCollins: Alison Klapthor, Aurora Parlagreco, Alison Donalty, and Barbara Fitzsimmons. All remaining gratitude goes to the publicity team's Elizabeth Ward and Stephanie Hoover, and School and Library Marketing's Patty Rosati.

These books would not exist without the support and encouragement from my amazing family and friends. Really. Thank you. To Mom, Dad, Whitney, Matt, employees of Dinkel's Bakery, the Reno family, and the city of Kent, Ohio—I aim to make you all proud.

Jeff Miller is a tall drink of water from Kent, Ohio. He is a big fan of snow, camping, taking steps two at a time, and LeBron James—but he likes writing books best. He lives and performs in Chicago, where he tells funny stories about working at summer camps and drinking far too much lake water as a child. You can follow him on Twitter @jeffmillerbooks or by visiting www.jeffmillerbooks.com.

FOLLOW ALL THE
NERDY ADVENTURES!